PHANTOMS AND FAIRIES

FROM NORWEGIAN FOLKLORE

BY
TOR ÅGE BRINGSVÆRD

✦

TRANSLATED BY
PAT SHAW

WOODCUTS BY
HANS GERHARD SÖRENSEN

TANUM-NORLI – OSLO

Second impression 1979
© Forlaget Tanum-Norli A/S 1979
ISBN 82-518-0853-7
Dreyer Aksjeselskap

PHANTOMS AND FAIRIES
FROM NORWEGIAN FOLKLORE

THE HIDDEN NORWEGIANS

Officially Norway has some 4 million inhabitants, but the real number is far greater. From times immemorial this country has been peopled by a host of curious creatures, sometimes visible, sometimes invisible. But they are not registered by the census taker and you will look for them in vain in the telephone book. They are The Hidden Norwegians.

The visitor who would like to have a glimpse of them must go about it very carefully. Neither police nor tourist information office can give any help, and travellers' cheques are not taken. He enters a world with a different set of rules, where black is white and in is out. In the big mountain hall of Dovregubben, the troll of trolls, he will be scratched in the eye by a splinter of rock, an operation which gives him a second sight, a new view of his surroundings. A mountain is no longer just a mountain, it is also the dwelling of trolls and giants. Through the din of the waterfall he will hear a trembling violin. It is the mysterious fiddler, the Fossegrim, who is playing. And by the river with the moss-grown stones he will see three beautiful maidens with cow-tails who want him for partner in a wild and wanton dance.

But don't forget the time! An hour with the hidden people may equal a week, even a year among ordinary humans. Many a troll-taken visitor has come back after what he believes to be a few hours and discovered that he has been declared lost and dead and that his wife has married again.

This book is meant to be a guide for everyone who wishes to meet the hidden people, the strange beings who live on in Norwegian lore and literature and in the subconscious depths of the national character. In addition to good advice, you will find descriptions of the best known characters. Read them carefully. It will save you a lot of trouble and unnecessary misunderstandings.

Tor Åge Bringsværd.

Contents

THE HULDER
AND THE HULDREFOLK

*Those not revealed shall remain
concealed . . . .*

The *huldrefolk* ('the hidden people') – also called the *un-
derjordiske* ('those under the ground'), the *haugfolk* ('people
of the mounds'), the *bergfolk* ('people of the hills') or *tusse-
folk* – dwell in mountains and mounds. They resemble ordinary people, but are often described as being somewhat
smaller in size, and the huldre women usually have a cow's
tail and a hollow back.

In many respects, their world is a reflection of our own.
The huldrefolk have farms with houses and cultivated fields,
and numerous herds of cattle that graze at night and are
tended by their own dairymaids and black dogs. They have
their own kings and clergymen and churches. A *haugbu*
('mound-dweller') is born, marries and dies exactly like
anyone else. Often the hidden people are said to possess
great riches. Everything there is supposed to be much finer
and more magnificent than with us. They are especially
rich in silver.

It is generally believed that the wild animals of forest and
field are the domestic animals of the huldrefolk. A huldre
man or woman can, for example, call the bear 'my hog'.
Similarly, the sea – and all the fish and other edible things
in it – is interpreted as the storehouse of the hidden people.
Thus, a hunter or fisherman *takes* something that belongs
to *them*. Certain fishing lakes were regarded as the special
property of the huldrefolk. No one else was permitted to
fish there. Such lakes were often called 'huldre tarns', and
the tradition maintains that they had a double bottom. A

distinct group of legends tells of courageous men who obtained permission to fish in a huldre tarn. They scattered earth from a graveyard in a ring around the water. The huldrefolk can neither enter nor leave such a circle, and the legends usually end with the two parties coming to terms.

Veins of silver and gold, and buried treasure were also regarded as the property of the huldrefolk. According to popular Norwegian belief, a blue light is supposed to shine over hidden treasures. (A blue light can also warn of death, or the fact that the hidden people dwell there). Treasure seekers were hindered in every conceivable way. The huldrefolk caused the most preposterous and terrifying hallucinations, so that anyone who wanted to be a successful treasure hunter had to have good nerves.

The religion of the huldrefolk is that of the Old Testament. Thus, they are not Christians, but they are not heathens either. They have their own clergymen and churches, and the hope of life eternal in Heaven after death.

The legends about the origins of the huldrefolk are often connected with the conception of Adam's two marriages. In the Book of Genesis (Chapter 1) it is written that God created man and woman, but no mention is made of Eve until the second chapter. The huldrefolk are descended from the children Adam had with his *first* wife, Lilith. According to another explanation, the huldrefolk are descended from the children Adam and Eve once tried to conceal, when Our Lord dropped in on them unexpectedly, the reason being that the children, on that occasion, were unkempt. Another version maintains that Adam and Eve were somewhat embarassed by the fact that they had so *many* children. And Our Lord, who sees everything, exclaimed in His wise wrath:

'Those not revealed shall remain concealed!'

As has been said, the huldre world is a reflection of our own. And this is also true in the sense that many things are the exact *opposite* of what we are accustomed to. And there

14   is another important difference – time passes so unreasonably quickly:

There was a man who was going out to chop timber. He took along enough food to last him for a week. He came to the shack in the evening. When he had eaten, a tusse came in.
'You're so alone,' said the tusse. 'Don't you think it's dull?'
'Oh, sometimes it is and sometimes it isn't,' said the man.
'We're having a wedding at home,' said the tusse, 'so come along with me!'
'That would have been fun,' said the man, 'but I dare not,' he said.
'You may come if you like,' said the tusse. So he accompanied him.
He had not gone far, before they reached the wedding farm. The room was full of people. They fiddled and danced and drank. The fiddler had a seat up on the wall; the bridegroom had a broken jaw. They were extremely hospitable. The man ate and drank a great deal. Otherwise he did nothing else but sleep. He kept this up for a good while. Then he asked the tusse to accompany him back to the shack. And the tusse went with him.
'How long do you think you've been gone?' he asked.
'I'd say a week,' replied the man.
'You've been gone for half a year,' said the tusse. Then the man was horror-stricken.
People had searched hard for him, but not a footprint nor a track was to be found. Then they thought he had changed his shape or had run away. Thus, when he came back, they were astounded.

The story is reminiscent of the legend that was told throughout Europe about a monk named Felix – the monk who went out in the forest for a few minutes, to listen to the birds singing in Paradise, and who did not return to the monastary until many generations later. Or, according to the Norwegian folktale 'Friends in Life and Death': a bridegroom, on his very wedding day, pays a visit to the Realm of the Dead with his deceased friend, and returns after what seems to be a couple of hours, but which turns out to be centuries. Whoever visits the huldre realm crosses

the threshold to another dimension. A visit can be tempting,
but is extremely dangerous.

Human beings and huldrefolk live invisibly side by side. But the dividing-line between the two worlds is no wall – if anything, it is a mist or a veil. Now and then the veil is lifted to one side – there is a break in the 'fog' – and representatives of the two parallel worlds confront one another. It is also generally believed that the invisibility of the huldrefolk is due to a magic cloak or hat, that makes the wearer invisible.

It paid to remain on good terms with one's invisible neighbors. It was especially important to respect the wishes of the hidden people for peace and quiet in the evening, and a night's rest. No one was supposed to make noise or speak in a loud voice after the sun had gone down. People were especially careful at the *seter* (the mountain summer dairy farm). Here, according to a report from Valdres, they went about and spoke only in whispers in the evening.

People preferred not go out of doors after it was dark. Even the animals had to be quiet. When the cows were let into the stall in the evening, care was taken to stuff wisps of grass in the bells or block them with a twig. Anyone who ignored the desire of the huldrefolk for quiet in the evening was severely punished. Most often, the punishment befell the cattle. Storaker has recorded the following formula from Strinda: 'After dark, people at the seter must not utter a single word aloud in the vicinity of the stall, so that the Tusses shall not harm the cattle by letting them milk blood, or making them sick in any other way.'

When people were going to build a new house – especially up at the seter – it paid to build it on a spot where the hidden people did not already have *their* own house. For this reason, one had to see to it that the house did not 'stand in anyone's way'. There were many ways of finding this out: if one tapped the cornerstone three times with a stick from a wild briar, one would discover if people were living underneath. A special sound was supposed to come from stones that were lying on top of a huldre dwelling. In some places, people usually went to sleep on the site they had chosen for themselves. If they slept soundly, the spot was quiet and safe. It was also a common test to leave behind an implement – usually an axe – on the site. If they were not supposed to build there, the huldrefolk came during the night and moved the axe to a spot where they could build.

If people were not on the lookout for such things *before* they built, it could happen that there might be so much trouble afterwards that they would be forced to tear down the whole house and move it to another spot. And the fact that the huldrefolk often had good reasons for demanding that a building be moved, is revealed in this legend from Østerdal:

On a farm here, there was a man who had the skinniest horses in spite of everything. No matter how well he looked after them, they were as spindle-shanked as ever. Then it happened, one Christmas Eve, that the man was going out in the barn to give the animals some fodder for the night. He was scarcely inside the door, when the floor seemed to open up beneath his feet, and he sank straight down until he came into a hall. And this hall was so fine that it was downright wicked. A table there was set with food of every description, and the man was invited over to the table to help himself. At first he said, 'No thank you', because he had not journeyed very far. But they felt that as long as he had come there, he could just as well taste what had been set out. He couldn't just leave without partaking of the Christmas fare – not when it was Christmas Eve, so he let them find a seat for him by the table. But it was not food that he could swallow. The food was of the best quality, it was. But everything he put in his mouth tasted of dung, and it was so rank that he was unable to swallow a bite.

'Well, now you can see how it is,' said a man who appeared to be the head of the household. 'Our food is always spoiled like that. No matter how we fix it, it's always uneatable. It runs down from your stall and into our food, so we're more than at a loss. But if you'll move your stall, then we'll both benefit from it.

You'll be able to enjoy your horses and we'll be able to enjoy
our food.'

'Yes, I can do that, all right,' said the man, 'but I don't
think I can start with it before Christmas is over.' No, they
didn't expect him to, either, as long as he would start on it then.

Yes, so he would, and at once he was standing up in the stall
again. Immediately after Christmas, he started on the work as
he had promised. From that day, there was never anything
wrong with his horses again, and it was as if good fortune had
settled over the farm once more.

Nowhere were there as many huldrefolk as at the seter
and in the surrounding neighborhood. This was interpreted in two ways – according to the first: the huldrefolk lived
at the seter as invisible doppelgangers. According to the
second: they did not live there at the same time as ordinary
people did, but moved in when the farmers went home in
the autumn, and yielded their place to them again when
they moved back up to the seter in the spring.

The first interpretation is at the bottom of the custom
that was practiced throughout Valdres, namely, that one
was supposed to shout a warning before emptying out boil-
ing water or anything else that was hot, in order that the
hidden people could get out of the way. But, in all likelihood, the most common conception was the one that the
huldrefolk dwelled at the seter most of the year, but with-
drew during the summer weeks when people were living
there. Thus it was the custom, when people moved into the
the seter with their cattle, that they respectfully greeted
the hidden people, and asked to be allowed to stay there for
a certain length of time. When they moved back home,
they politely thanked the hidden people for their stay. It
was not advisable to remain longer at the seter than had been
agreed upon. There were not many who dared to be on bad
terms with the huldrefolk, which is what happened if the
farmer did not keep his part of the bargain.

There are also many examples of people and huldrefolk
living peacefully and tolerantly together, rendering mutual

2 – Phantoms.

services to one another. For the most part, these were services connected with the daily work. But it also happened that people were asked for help in rendering more unusual assistance, and received abundant payment for it. Many legends tell of someone who had lent a hand during a childbirth in the huldre home.

The huldrefolk stood shoulder to shoulder with their human neighbors in difficult situations. Along the Swedish border, it even happened that they mustered their own companies of huldre soldiers, when Norway was threatened by war.

This account, about the huldrefolk taking part in the war of 1814, was told to Ola Svea by his father:

If a man fell in the ranks, and there was no one to take his place, a stranger came and lay down and started to shoot. And this fellow bore a charmed life – they saw it time after time.

There was a company that chanced upon the Swedes on the eastern bank of the river, outside Vinger. They charged right away, because there did not seem to be any more Swedes. They chased them out onto a flat meadow, while some of the others moved up on the sides and were going to ring them in.

But they were ringed in themselves, because no sooner were they down on the meadow and were about to attack the Swedes, than they were fired upon from the edge of the forest. And all at once the meadow was swarming with Swedes on three sides, and on the fourth side was the river. And they themselves were standing on the flat meadow without so much as a stone to crawl behind.

They were going to try to fight their way through and go up in the woods, when they heard the big drum start to beat up on the hill. They thought the Norwegians were on their way to help, and started shouting, 'Hurrah!' And the Swedes thought so too, because they took to their heels and headed south along the edge of the forest as fast as they could. And the Norwegians went after them. They knew that their own men were up on the hill, and they ran along the edge of the forest and shot at the Swedes.

The ones who were at the very bottom of the hill could not catch up with the Swedes anyway, so they were sent up the hill to meet the soldiers who were coming that way. They took a

cow path up, but there was no one to be found. They stopped
and listened for the drum, but there was nothing to be heard.
They couldn't understand it, because they should have been
there by then. After all, it had to be their own men they had
heard, they couldn't just have been hearing things – not the
whole company. And the Swedes had also taken to their heels
because of them, and those fellows didn't leave until things
looked serious. Why, they had the whole company ringed in.

So they sat down and pondered over it. All at once they
heard the drum again, louder and louder. They jumped up, and
saw a whole company heading north. But to their astonishment,
the company came marching through the most impenetrable
wilderness as easily as if they were on the most level road. And
when they had come abreast of them, they saw that they were
not dressed like other soldiers, but were wearing clothes that
had gone out of use a long time ago. Then the onlookers realized
what manner of soldiers they were. The huldrefolk had helped
them out. Things would have turned out badly, if they hadn't
taken part.

Up to now, we have concerned ourselves with what can be
called the brighter side of the relationship between human
beings and the huldrefolk. We have seen how the farmers
have tried to make the best of cohabitation with their dangerous and invisible neighbors. But people can also adopt
a different attitude. Instead of bowing to the hidden powers, they can take up the fight, drive the hidden people
away in order to gain control of the land for themselves.
Because, in all fairness, the huldrefolk are dangerous and
unpredictable neighbors, and no matter how well they are
treated, one can never rely too much on sorcery and witchcraft. Whenever someone defies them, they become dangerous both to people and their livestock. And when mortals
rise up in open conflict, it can often turn into a life-and-
death struggle.

In this struggle, man has three powerful weapons: the
names of Jesus and God, fire and steel. Steel was especially
effective. Not only did it chase the opponents away, but
many people have also become a cow richer by throwing a

knife or an axe over a cow belonging to the huldrefolk. Indeed, some people have even acquired a whole farm in this way. Like the huldrefolk themselves, many of their possessions had the quality of invisibility. But if one were able to throw steel over the object, the spell was broken. Then it became visible forever, and the huldrefolk were powerless to demand it back.

Along the Norwegian coastline there are a number of islands that originally belonged to the huldrefolk. They have been 'discovered' in that someone has brought fire or steel there. Often it was said that the one who came with the steel would be changed to stone as punishment. For this reason, it was the custom to send a domestic animal first – usually with a pair of scissors fastened around its neck. Legends about such huldre islands are often attached to the conception of 'The Fortunate Islands' – a Utopia in the sea, which was only visible and accessible to seamen in the greatest danger of being shipwrecked. The best known of these islands is *Utröst*, in Lofoten.

All kinds of injuries and accidents, which could not be explained, were interpreted as being caused by the hidden people. If anything happened to the cattle, the hidden people received the blame. If someone lost a cow, it was said at once that the huldrefolk had stolen it. When the cow was found – half-starved and exhausted – it was clear to everyone how gruesome the hidden people could be. The animals could also have changed color somewhat. In Lofoten and Vesterålen, it was regarded as a sign that the animal had been taken by the haugfolk if it had acquired a darker, a bluish hue. The change in color was usually explained as the brand used by the hidden people for marking the animal.

The hidden people not only steal animals, they are also kidnappers. There are many legends about children who have been snatched from their cradles and carried inside a mound or a mountain.

Adults can also be lured into a mountain. Shepherds and others who frequent forests and mountains could become lost in a way that was regarded as unusual or unnatural. The only possible explanation appeared to be that they had been carried off by the hidden people. Most legends tell of instances in which the mountain sojourn lasts for only a short time, and the missing person returns to the parish and tells what has happened. There are even examples of people testifying before a court. From Romsdal we have a description of such an inquiry. Here it was verified by witnesses, and by the court, that a girl had been lured into the mountain by the hidden people. In court she described how it looked inside the mountain, and no one doubted her story.

Such legends contain a number of similarities. We hear that the hidden people are powerless in the face of *steel*. It can also help to have a Bible, a hymnbook or a catechism in one's bosom. They also want to force or tempt the person into *eating and drinking*. It is important that he resist this temptation, no matter how hungry and thirsty he may be. If he succumbs, he is lost and must remain inside the mountain for the rest of his life. The hidden people are *afraid of church bells*. Whenever someone was lured into the mountain, the church bells were always rung. If the mountain lay beyond the range of hearing, it happened that the church bells were taken down from the steeple and transported to the spot where the person was believed to sit captive. In this way, many people have been 'rung out of the mountain'. It was also generally believed that the person *becomes mentally ill* after he has been released again. In most cases, the person recovers after a while – but often in such a way that it is noticeable that he is not completely normal.

Most legends tell about people who return, but there are also a number of accounts about people who remain inside the mountain forever. The curiosity to find out how people

22 live inside the mountain finds its expression in legends about brief encounters with them, at which time information from and about them is received. We often hear of captured maidens getting married and having babies in their huldre home.

It probably happened very often that the dairymaids at the seter were visited by young men who were out courting. But human beings were not the only ones who paid such visits. Huldre lads also came courting. There are a number of legends in which not only the wooing itself is described, but also the arts that were employed in order to get rid of the tusse suitor. Among a number of good remedies, it may be mentioned, that it was supposed to help if a soldier in full trappings could be persuaded to sleep with the girl for three nights in a row!

Nonetheless, it often happened that the tusse suitor almost managed to trick the girl. Here is a legend that was written down by Peter Chr. Asbjörnsen, the Norwegian folklorist:

One summer, a long long time ago, they were up at the seter with the cows from Melbustad, in Hadeland. But they hadn't been there long before the cows became so restless that it was downright impossible to control them. Many girls tried herding them, but matters did not improve until a girl who had just plighted her troth came to work for them. Then the cows were calm right away, and were no longer difficult to herd. She stayed up at the seter alone, and had no other living soul with her than her dog.

One afternoon, as she was sitting inside the seter, she thought her sweetheart came in and sat down beside her and started talking about having the wedding right away. But she sat quite still and did not answer a word, for she seemed to feel somewhat strange. Little by little, people began to come in, and they started to set the table with silver and food, and bridesmaids carried in a crown and a beautiful wedding gown, which they dressed her in. And they placed the crown upon her head, as was the custom in those days, and rings were put on her fingers.

She thought she knew all the people who had come. There

were women from the farms and girls her own age. But the dog had certainly noticed that something was wrong. It ran away, straight down to Melbustad, and there it whined and barked, giving them no peace until they followed it back again.

Then the boy who was her sweetheart took his gun and went up to the seter. When he came to the yard, it was filled with saddled horses. He sneaked over to the cottage, and peeked through a crack in the door at those who were sitting inside. It was easy to tell that they were trolls and huldrefolk, and so he fired the gun over the door. At the same moment the door flew open, and one ball of grey wool after the other, each one bigger than the last, came rolling out, winding itself around his legs. When he got inside, the girl was sitting there dressed as a bride. He had come in the nick of time. Only the ring for the little finger was lacking, and then she would have been ready.

'For Christ's sake! What's going on here?' he asked, looking about. All the silver was still on the table, but all the good food had turned into moss and toadstools and cow dung and toads, and other things like that.

'What does all this mean?' he asked. 'Why are you sitting here dressed as a bride?'

'You should ask!' said the girl. 'You've been sitting here talking to me about the wedding all afternoon.'

'No, I came just now,' he said. 'It must have been someone who made himself look like me.'

Then she began to come to herself again, but she was not really well for a long time afterward. She told him that she thought that both he and the whole party had been there. He took her down to the village right away so that nothing more could happen to her, and they held the wedding at once while she was still wearing the wedding finery of the huldrefolk. The crown and all the finery were hung up at Melbustad, and they are supposed to be there to this very day.

Otherwise, it was mostly at Christmas-time that the huldrefolk and other spirits were abroad. A considerable group of legends tells about huldrefolk who visit an isolated farm in order to celebrate Christmas. It often happens that the farmer and his family are forced to vacate the premises as long as the hidden people are around playing havoc. This repeats itself year after year, until a man finally arrives –

usually a chance wayfarer – who not only dares to remain under the same roof with the huldrefolk, but also manages to frighten them away. Best known of these legends is 'The Tabby Cat on Dovre Mountain', which is about the legendary hero Per Gynt. In this story, Per has a polar bear with him, and it is really the bear that frightens away the hidden people.

The most celebrated of all the huldrefolk is the *hulder*. This is the way she was described by clergyman Andreas Faye, in his collection of Norwegian legends from 1833 – the first collection of legends in Norway:

Round about the countryside there are legends about a supernatural being called the hulder, which keeps to forests and mountains. This creature looks like a beautiful woman. She generally wears a white skirt and a white kerchief, but, in addition, she has a cow's tail, that she can roll up or let hang down as she sees fit. When she comes among mortals, whose company she generally seeks, she carefully conceals her long tail. She is especially fond of handsome young men, with whom she likes to dance.

Once she appeared at a gathering where everyone wanted to dance with the beautiful young stranger. But while they were dancing, the one who was dancing with her caught sight of her long tail. He realized at once that he was dancing with a hulder, and became frightened. He regained his composure at once, and said to her alone: 'Fair maiden, you're losing your garter.' She vanished at once, but she later rewarded the considerate and discreet young lad with beautiful gifts and good breeding cattle.

Because she can change herself into the fairest of maidens and promise the lads the moon, she is far more dangerous to men than the huldre men are to young maidens. Whoever has anything to do with a hulder maiden, finds it difficult to get rid of her again, as she is with him when he least desires or expects it. If the lad's intentions are honorable, then she usually lets herself be christened and lets the marriage banns be published. And during the christening or the wedding ceremony, her long tail falls off.

Sometimes the infatuated hulder will take a young man inside the mountain with her. But if he should happen to say, 'Jesus' name', then neither the hulder nor anyone else can have any power over him. Nonetheless, the one who has been lured inside the mountain will always retain a mental or bodily injury.

We have read that the hulder dressed in white, but green or blue clothing was just as common.

Why does the hulder seek the company of human males? Her motives are undoubtably the same as those behind the abduction into the mountains and the kidnapping of newborn babies – a desire to introduce fresh blood into the race. Human beings live in sunshine and light. In spite of everything, they are perhaps thought of as being more powerful than the hidden people, who shuffle about in eternal twilight and darkness. For this reason, the hulder maiden and the hulder lad want to mingle their blood with that of human beings, to have children with them.

The word 'powerful' was used, but the hulder is no delicate young maiden herself:

The hulder once showed herself to a man who was standing in a forest, splitting a big trunk of a pine tree. She tried to make him fall in love with her – she spoke to him kindly and seated herself on the trunk right in front of him, so he could see how beautiful she was. All the same, he noticed that she had a long tail, which she concealed in the crack in the trunk. Then it occurred to him to loosen a big wedge that stood in the middle of the trunk. Now when he knocked this wedge loose, the cleft snapped together so the hulder's tail was caught fast. Then she became frightened and ran away. And she was so strong that she dragged the trunk with her, and tore down a lot of the forest before she was able to free herself.

Many legends tell about this supernatural strength. The hulder can bend iron with her bare hands as easily as anything. But back to this business of being 'boy-crazy'. Here is a fragment of a legend from Hardanger:

There was a man who spent a lot of time up in the mountains fishing and hunting during the spring and autumn. One evening he was sitting in the hunting shack grilling reindeer meat on the coals. All at once, his wife came in through the door (or so he thought).

'You're trying to starve us,' she said.

'What are you saying, wife?' asked the man.

'You took the storehouse key with you, when you left,' she said.

The man started digging in his pockets, and there he found the key.

'It's too late for you to go home tonight,' said the man. 'You'd better stay here until tomorrow morning.'

'Yes, I guess I'd better,' she replied. With that she started getting undressed. But as she was going to climb up in the bed, he noticed that she had a tail hanging down from her rear end.

'Hide your whip-lash, wife!' cried the man.

Then she jumped down to the floor and was out of the shack as if she'd been burnt.

The man grabbed the meat from the coals and threw it after her. It landed on her bare bottom, just as she popped out through the door.

Then a loud laughter was heard – it echoed from the mountains all around – and a voice could be heard crying: 'Ragnhild Steak-rump! Ragnhild Steak-rump! That's what you get for being such a hussy!'

This time things turned out well, but it could have been worse:

There are many legends about hulders who have visited charcoal burners. Old Ola Heldal, he was burning charcoal up at Ostebakkje, below Åsebru. A hulder came to him one evening and pretended to be his wife. And he thought she was, too.

'But, my dear, how did you manage to get up here?'

'Oh, I just wanted to come up and see how you were getting on.'

'But how did you get away from the children?' he asked.

'Oh, I managed to get someone to look after them,' she replied. She slept with him the whole night, but when she left in the morning, he caught sight of her tail. – He told about this himself. – She kissed him that night too, he said, but at the same time she gave his chin a lick with her tongue, and he regretted it ever since, for his beard never grew there again.

Nonetheless, he was lucky to escape with nothing worse than a beardless chin. In Sweden there was a time when sexual relations with the hulder were punishable by death, and, incredibly enough, a number of men are said to have confessed their crime. In Norway we are far more humane. Here we even allow the hulder to marry, and, as a rule, she makes a good wife.

In conclusion, here is a legend about a man from Telemark named Sveinong Vreim. He had a child by a hulder, but he did not know it:

At Vreim, in Böhæra, a long time ago, there lived a man named Sveinong. Once he was up on Lifjell looking for his horses. He came to a big, splendid farm in the midst of the most desolate mountains. As far as he knew there wasn't supposed to be a farm there, so it had to be a huldre farm. But he was so tired that he had to go inside all the same. A woman and a little girl were there.

'Good evening,' said Sveinong.

'Good evening,' said the woman. 'Are you out looking for your horses?'

Yes, he was.

'You'd better go down in the cellar and tap some ale,' said the woman to the little girl.

'Shall I take it from the barrel the cat is sitting on?' she asked.

'Are you out of your mind, girl? Do you want to kill your father?' said the woman.

'Father did you say?' said Sveinong. 'Am *I* her father?'

'Yes, don't you remember the time you were sleeping in the loft at Vreim, and you dreamt you were embracing a woman? Well, that woman was me, and this is your child,' said the woman, and pointed to the girl who came with the bowl of ale. Well, Sveinong drank, and he was given food too, and they took good care of him. But then he saw that the girl had only one eye, and so he asked:

'The girl has only one eye? How did that happen?'

'Oh, you did that,' said the woman.

'I did?'

'Yes, you did. Don't you remember the time you were standing by the chopping block to chop wood, and a whirlwind blew up? And it's the custom to throw knives at it, but one shouldn't do that, because those are our children who are dancing. You threw your knife at it, and hit your daughter in the eye. Since then she has had only one eye.'

The next morning the woman told him where to find his horses. 'But you mustn't look back when you're riding home.'

Well, Sveinong found his horses and was going to ride home. But he couldn't help it, he had to look back. And then the horse was seen to fall on its hindlegs down into a lake – he had been riding over a big tarn up there.

TROLLS

As big as mountains,
as stupid as a cow.

Trolls (jutuls, riser) occupy a central position in the Norwegian folktales. Big and stupid – and surrounded by tremendous riches – they survey the world from their almost inaccessible mountain strongholds. Again and again, we hear of valiant peasant lads setting out to rescue princesses, who have been lured into the mountain. Trolls are naive and easy to fool, but they are strong – and thirsty for the blood of a Christian man. The lad has to drink a magic potion before he is able to swing the troll-sword and chop off the monster's heads. Yes, heads – because a Norwegian troll does not have only one head. The average is three – and they are equally as thick-skulled.

We also hear about trolls in the Medieval ballads. Here the trolls dwell in a separate realm – they are a race apart, in a land far to the north or northeast. This land is called *Trollebotn, Juskehei* or *Skomehei*, and is wreathed in eternal twilight and darkness. Even where such a land is not named outright, the trolls that visit the realm of mortals are usually said to come from the north.

Heroes set out on quests to this unpleasant, twilight land, either to rescue a captured maiden or, pure and simple, to kill time – and a couple of trolls into the bargain. Killing trolls was a widely accepted pastime among the ancient Norsemen – if we are to believe the ballads. Our national saint, King Olav, is said to have been especially skilled in this profession.

Trolls are gigantic, and repulsive to look at. Most often they are clad in skins. Their noses are long and crooked, and their eyes are as big as pools of water. When a troll walks on solid ground, it looks as if it is wading in a mire. It treads so heavily that it sinks down, sometimes all the way up to its knees.

In the folktales trolls eat human flesh, and such a conception is not foreign to the ballads either.

At sea, trolls sail about in boats of iron or stone. They are usually out wandering at Christmas time, and this is often the time when the heroes set out to do battle with them. As a rule, trolls do not possess any particular weapons. They use whatever they happen to have at hand: big stones, which they throw, and trees, which they pull up by the roots and strike out wildly with. However, it is sometimes mentioned that trolls fight with huge iron bars.

But these are the trolls of the folktales and ballads, who have long since disappeared from popular Norwegian belief. In this book we are concerned with the true trolls of the *legends*. The most important difference between a legend and a folktale is that the folktale *(eventyr)* was told for entertainment, whereas the legend *(sagn)* was believed and regarded as a true account from real life. And, in the legends, the trolls receded more and more into the background. The existing material is very scanty, and most of the troll-legends are attached to certain phenomena that are supposed to be *reminders* of the time when the trolls were playing havoc. Footprints on bare rock reveal how big they have been. Enormous boulders, which lie by themselves and which no one understands how they came there, are explained as having been thrown by trolls. Now and then, the trolls themselves are standing there too, because, in the legends as in the folktales, trolls must try to avoid daylight. They are turned to stone by the rays of the sun. But this can also happen as the result of reciprocal magic...

On Hestemand Island, at Lurö in Nordland, there is a mountain which, at a distance, resembles a knight wearing a

flowing cape. In olden times, this mountain was a jutul who lived here. At the same time, there was a maiden who lived on Lek Island, in Namdalen, some seventy miles to the south, and here he went courting. But she was so high and mighty that she scornfully turned him down. And, in addition, she was so skilled in the art of magic, that she changed all of his messengers into stone – and they can still be seen as skerries around the northern tip of the island. Furious at such behavior, the jutul bent his bow in order to avenge this insult. The mighty arrow sped along, and went straight through a high mountain, *Torghatten* – where the great hole which the arrow bored through the solid rock can still be seen.

'It's making headway!' exclaimed the jutul. But as its speed was slackened by boring its way through Torghatten, the arrow did not quite reach its goal. It fell at the maiden's feet on the northern tip of Lek Island – where it still lies in the shape of a big, longish stone. With the help of reciprocal magic, they were both changed to stone. And here they are to sit and look at each other until Doomsday.

Even in our day, a Nordland wayfarer seldom sails past without doffing his cap to the Maiden of Lek Island.

Often the same legend was told about trolls and huldre-folk, and it is often impossible to determine which is the original. However, in those tales in which *size* is the point of the story, we can assume that it is a legend about a troll:

At Vinje, in Telemark, there is a lake called Totak which seldom freezes over before Christmas. By this lake, on Vaa farm, there once lived a man named Dyre Vaa, and he was renowned for not being afraid of anything on earth. It happened late one Christmas Eve, that the people at Vaa heard a terrible hollering on the other side of the lake. The others became frightened, but Dyre walked calmly down to the water to find out what was going on. He took his boat and rowed over to the spot where the sound was coming from. Despite the darkness, he could tell that the hollering came from a huge mountain troll, even though he was unable to see it. The troll asked at once who it was.

'It's Dyre Vaa,' he replied, and then he asked the troll where it had come from.

'From Aashaug,' came the reply.

'And where are you going?' continued Dyre.

'To Glomshaug, to my maidens. Will you ferry me across?' asked the troll.

Dyre promised to do so, but when the troll put its foot in the boat, it nearly sank.

'Make yourself lighter, you big old troll!' yelled Dyre.

'Yes, I'll make myself lighter,' replied the troll.

Now as they were rowing across the lake, Dyre said: 'Let me see how big you are.'

'No I won't,' said the troll, 'but I'll leave a sign in the rowboat.'

Early on Christmas morning, Dyre went down to the lake to look for the promised sign, and in the boat he found the thumb of the Troll's mitten. He took it home and measured it – and it wasn't tiny – it held two unstinted bushels.

Yes, trolls are enormous. They wade across the deepest lakes and step over high ridges. In the rock they have hollowed out huge potholes in which they cook their food and wash their young. Such potholes can be seen in all parts of Norway. Their cows are not very small either. In Telemark, a troll-cow was once seen standing on the top of a mountain. It leaned over the edge and drank from the lake below.

Trolls hate churches and the sound of church bells. Both trolls and troll hags do their best to crush the churches under rockslides or with a lucky throw of a boulder.

But church bells are not the only things they dislike. In a mountain near Bergen there once lived a troll who often appeared at night with flashing eyes. The story goes that it once rolled huge stones after a herd of cattle because the tinkling of the cowbells got on its nerves. The cowherd saw it clearly.

A relatively large group of legends – apparently self-contradictory – tells about trolls that *build* a church. But this becomes all the more understandable when we learn of the unparalleled remuneration which the troll has stipulated for itself:

The cathedral in Trondheim is renowned far and wide as one of Christianity's most remarkable churches. It was especially magnificent in the old days, when it had its towering spire. St.

3 – Phantoms.

Olav was able to build the church all right, but to put up the spire was beyond his strength. In his dilemma, St. Olav promised the sun to anyone who would undertake the task of setting it up. But there was no one who dared or was able to do it, until a troll came who lived in Ladehammer – a mountain just outside the city. He promised to undertake the task for the payment that had been promised, and also on the condition that St. Olav was not to call him by name, if he ever managed to find out what it was. St. Olav had now gotten himself into a perplexing situation, as far as his promise was concerned, and so he tried to pick up a clue as to the troll's name.

Thus it happened one night, around midnight, that St. Olav sailed past Ladehammer, and when he came to a spot that is still called *Kjerringa*, (the Hag), he heard a child crying inside the mountain. The mother comforted it and promised it the 'heavenly gold' (the sun) when Tvester came home. St. Olav was overjoyed, and hurried back to the church. He got there just in time. The spire was already in place, and the troll was busy putting the last golden knob on the vane. Then St. Olav shouted:

'Tvester! You're putting the vane too far to the west!'

No sooner had the troll heard his name than he plunged down dead from the spire.

There are many variants of this legend, and they can all be traced back to an ancient Norse myth. According to the Snorri Edda, a jotun came to the Æsir (the gods) and offered to build a wall around Asgard. The wall was to be a protection against all evil, and he promised that it would be ready by a certain time. But he wanted the goddess Freya and the sun and the moon as payment if the wall were ready by the appointed time. The Æsir accepted the offer, for no one counted on his being able to manage it. The jotun set a murderous pace, and for a long time things looked bad. But then Loke changed himself into a mare and lured the jotun's stallion away, thereby delaying the work. Loke later gave birth to a foal with eight legs, *Sleipne*, which became Odin's horse.

THE CHANGELING

Why, this must be a troll-child!

The belief in the changeling has a tragic background, and stems from the desire of every parent to have healthy, normal children. A physical or mental handicap is not necessarily apparent immediately after the birth, but the day arrives when the parents are forced to admit that their child is 'different'. What are they to do then? Today people *accept* the truth, no matter how hard it may be to bear. Our forefathers chose to run away from it. It is difficult and painful for parents to realize that a child, which has apparently been healthy before, suddenly looks different. Can it be the same child? they asked. It hasn't been exchanged, has it?

We are not going to enter into a discussion of the nature of these illnesses here, but shall merely point out the tragic fact that, right up to the middle of the 19th century, sick and handicapped children in a number of instances were not accepted by their parents. Often they were cruelly mistreated as well.

The parents believed that their own child had been taken from them, and that the child they had gotten in its place was not even a human child. It was a child of the hidden people – a huldre- or tusse-child. The baby in the cradle was not their own – it was a *changeling*.

The purpose of the kidnapping was most likely to bring new blood into the race of trolls. We also know that in the ancient Norse myths it appears that trolls and jotuns felt the need for mingling their blood with that of mortals – indeed, with that of the gods as well. The same conception is probably at the bottom of all the legends about people who been carried off into the mountains.

But why do the hidden people leave their own child behind as compensation? Perhaps the tusse parents want to
give the child its share in the blessings of human life – with
the implication that mortals are more favorably situated
than the hidden people. In Setesdal they had a simpler
answer: The tusscs wanted to swap the child because it
was sick. And to most people this was probably a more
plausible reason. Besides, everyone could see for himself
that the changeling was unwell.

Thus, every woman in labor was afraid that her child
would be exchanged. She knew that the hidden people
would try to get hold of it, so it paid to take the necessary
precautions.

Before the christening, the child was regarded as a hea-
then, and, as such, was especially vulnerable to all kinds of
witchcraft. The christening, and the Christian faith, afford-
ed protection. For this reason, it was a good idea to have
the child christened as quickly as possible, usually on the
first Sunday when a sermon was scheduled after the birth.

During the critical period between the birth and the
christening, the child needed extra protection. It must never be left alone, neither by day nor by night. During the
night, one or preferably two adults had to watch over it,
and a candle always had to be lighted. The child must not
be taken out of doors before it was christened. And in
the event that anyone dared to do such a foolhardy thing,
great care had to be taken that the child had *steel* on its
body. There was also supposed to be a piece of steel in
the cradle – usually in the form of a knife or a pair of scissors. In Vest-Agder, a sheath knife was placed in the wall
above the cradle. Other protective objects were a prayer
book – often a page torn from the book would do – and
a piece of flatbread, because bread was 'Heaven-sent'. In
Ofoten, a cross was chalked over the door, and both here
and elsewhere in Norway the name of Jesus was supposed
to have protective powers.

The journey to the church to christen the child was regarded as especially hazardous. It was taken for granted that the powers of evil would make a last attempt to steal the child. Thus, during this journey, the child often had a silver spoon or a silver shilling sewed in its swaddling clothes. Silver was also believed to have protective powers. Nonetheless, people had the greatest faith in steel, and a large darning needle was usually fastened to the child's cap on the right side of its head.

'It has been my experience,' writes Landstad, *'that the pitiful crying of a child in the church, upon investigation, has been found to have been caused by the darning needle, which was deeply imbedded in the poor child's flesh.'*

But, despite every precaution, it can still happen that the child becomes a changeling. The description of the way a changeling looks is the same everywhere – not only here in Norway, but also in other countries where this belief has prevailed. Behind the legends we suspect a whole conglomeration of children's diseases, most of which are connected with malnutrition. In many instances, however, it is quite simply a deformed child which is called a changeling.

If one discovers that a child is a changeling, or even *suspects* it, steps are taken to recover the mother's own child – or at least to get rid of the changeling, which is often a terrible nuisance. As far as this latter problem was concerned: In Solör a magic formula was recited. It was believed that the child would die if it were a changeling. From Telemark we hear that a child that was suspect was held up naked to the sun on Easter morning. If it were a changeling it would burst, because, as we know, trolls cannot stand the rays of the sun!' In many places it was customary to *smöyge* (literally 'to thread') the child – in other words, to drag it through a hole in the ground or a hole or a cleft in a tree. In Hallingdal, at the same time, they used to fire a shot over the child's head in order to frighten it. Moreover, it was preferable that the one who did the shooting be a soldier, and, at the enemy.

People also tried to frighten the changeling in other ways: for example, by pretending they were thinking of throwing it on the fire or in a hot oven. The purpose was to frighten the changeling into revealing its true identity. When the changeling is exposed, it must disappear, and it is often possible to arrange an exchange with the hidden people. The changeling can also be *tricked* into revealing its identity. Thus, it is necessary to think up something unusual, something that will make the changeling express its amazement, or cause it to speak or laugh against its will. Then it is done for. Often it discloses the fact that, in reality, it has attained an unusually great age, for example that it can remember when a specific forest has burned down and grown up again three times!

When it has finally been established that there is a changeling in the house, it pays to contact the hidden people in order that one might perhaps get one's own child back again. There are examples of people exposing children at night in order to effect an exchange. From Nord-Hordaland, there is an account of a father who shouted in the forest that he was going to 'scour the forest, until the whole place shook' unless he got the right child back again. Then he put the changeling down on the ground, and the huldre came and put his own child in its stead.

But, as a rule, one does not get very far in this world with threats – and not with the hidden people either. Thus the most customary practice is to tease and abuse the changeling in the hope that the hidden people will feel sorry for it and relinquish the human child.

In 'A Wise Woman', Peter Chr. Asbjörnsen tells about a changeling at Joramo farm in Lesja:

'My great-great-grandmother was at Joramo, in Lesja, and she had a changeling. I never saw him, for she was dead and he was gone long before I was born. But my mother told me about him. He had the face of a weather-beaten old man. He had red eyes like a carp, and they glowed in the dark like an owl. His head was as long as a horse's head and as big as a cabbage. But his legs were like the legs of a sheep and his body was like last year's dried meat. All he ever did was bawl and howl and yell, and if he got his hands on anything, he would throw it straight in his mother's face. He was always as hungry as a hound dog. He would eat anything he saw, and he practically ate them out of house and home. The older he grew, the angrier he became, and there was no end to his yelling and screeching. But they were never able to make him utter a single word. He was the nastiest troll that anyone had ever heard of, and they had trouble with him both night and day. They sought advice here and there, and his mother was advised to do first one thing and then the other. But she didn't have the heart to thrash him before she was really certain that he was a changeling. But then someone told her to say that the king was coming. Then she was supposed to light a big fire on the hearth and break an egg. She was to hang the shell over the fire, and put the measuring rod down through the chimney pipe. Well, she did as she was told. When the changeling caught sight of this, he stood up in the cradle and stared at it. The woman went out and peered in through the keyhole. Then he crawled out of the cradle on his hands – but his legs were lying up in the cradle – and he stretched himself out, and he became so long, yes, so long that he reached all the way across the floor and all the way up in the hearth.

'Well,' he said. 'I'm so old now that I've seen Lesja forest grow up seven times, but never before have I seen such a big porridge stirrer in such a tiny cauldron at Joramo!'

When the woman saw and heard this, she'd had enough. Then she knew he was a changeling, and when she came back inside, he coiled up like a serpent over in the cradle. Then she started abusing him, and one Thursday evening she took him outside and gave him a real thrashing on the garbage heap. Then there was a whining and whimpering around her. The second Thursday evening went just like the first, but when she thought he'd had enough, she heard someone speak as if beside her, and she could tell that it was her own child:

'Every time you beat Tjøstul Gautstigen, they beat me inside the mountain.'

But on the third Thursday evening, she gave the changeling

another hiding. Then an old crone came flying up with a young-
ster, as quick as lightning.

'Hand over Tjøstul! Here's your whelp back again!' she said, and flung the child at her.

THE UTBURD

Father and mother have I none,
nor do I lie in consecrated ground

The *utburd* is also a ghost. The name is attributed to the Old Norse expression for exposing children – *at bera ut born* or *barna útburðr*. The custom of taking the lives of newborn babies, who did not seem strong enough to survive, has been well known, at one time or another, among almost all peoples. It is best known from Greece where the Spartans, under the Law of Lycurgus, reduced the whole thing to a system in order to create a strong race. Here in the North, the reasons were first and foremost crop failure and poverty. It could also be the child of a concubine, which the wife did not wish to have in the house, or a child whose mother had been abandoned by the father. Thus, we know that St. Olav, the king, was in danger of being exposed for this reason. Violence was seldom done to a child which someone wanted to get rid of in this way. Often the child was bundled in clothing, carried out to a deserted spot and placed in an open grave. Now and then, it was placed in a hole in the ground, under the roots of a tree, with a stone flag over it as protection against wild animals. A piece of pork was usually placed in the child's mouth, in order that it could have something to suck on – despite the fact that it was intended to starve to death...

Not a few children had their lives spared because someone happened to find and take care of them. The rearing of someone else's child was considered to be a meritorious deed, and, in addition, it was a good safeguard against witchcraft.

It was a disgrace to expose a child, and if it were abso-
lutely necessary, it had to be done before the child had been
put to the breast, and before it had been given a name. Otherwise it was regarded as murder.

Our early Christian decrees expressly forbade exposing
a child, whether it had been christened or not, *provided that*
it was not so deformed that it could not take nourishment.
Then it was supposed to be carried out in the forest, or lie
outside the church door, under the surveillance of a kins-
man, until it died.

While the Old Norse *útburðr* was the name of the exposed
child itself, the New Norwegian word *utburd*, or *utbor*, cor-
responds to the dead child's ghost. It is dangerous to encounter the utburd. It is a tormenting spirit in the truest sense
of the word. It can inflict sickness upon people. It hates all
human beings and pursues them along the roads, but it is
especially the mother it is looking for.

The utburd is notorious for the piercing cries it utters.
For this reason, it is often called *ropar* ('shrieker') or *gast*
('ghost'). In addition, both of these words are the names of
a bird, because the utburd often roams about in the shape
of a bird – usually an owl – and it utters horrible shrieks in
the evening and throughout the night. The shrieks often
resemble the grievous crying of a child, but sometimes they
can have a more menacing sound. The utburd can imitate
every sound, and mimic every animal.

There are divergent views as to the utburd's appearance.
In Verdal, the utburd is supposed to have been seen in the
shape of a tiny, naked child. In Nordland, it has appeared
as a human being without a throat, and with the hooves of
a sheep. In all likelihood, the absence of a throat refers to
the cause of death – by throttling. The same is true of the
legends in which the utburd appears with a kerchief or
hair ribbon around its neck. In Østerdal, a black dog has
been seen where the child was killed. Otherwise, the story
usually goes that the utburd can change its shape. It can

make itself so tiny that, like the mare, it can crawl through the keyhole, and it can make itself as big as a troll and reach all the way up to the roof of the cowshed.

The utburd does not become dangerous right away. Only after five years – others say three or seven – does it begin to make the roads unsafe. Often it clings to people's backs and weighs them down almost to their knees. If someone gets the utburd on his back while he is driving, the sleigh becomes so heavy that the horse is unable to pull it. It does not release its hold until it sees a light, or crosses running water – as in this legend from Helgeland:

The utburd was an irascible and disagreeable fellow who always attacked if he but had a chance. More often than not, he was invisible – only his shrieking and bellowing could be heard. In Bolvikbakken, up from Langfjord, an utburd hung out in the old days. Ole Eljaso, from Aslakaun, was working at Langfjord at that time. One evening, as he was on his way home to Aslakaun, the utburd came after him. He felt the way the earth was shaking, and realized at once that even though he was big and strong, he had met his match here. He ran for his life without daring to look back. If he looked back, he would be bewitched and not come off the spot – this he knew – and then he would have the utburd upon him at the next moment. But the utburd came closer and closer, and when he had come to the Syli River, he expected to be caught at any moment. But then he made one last effort, and jumped in the river with a mighty splash and came across. Then he was saved, because the utburd never dared to cross water. But Ole was so afraid that he dared not stop until he came to Elvgarden. Only then did he dare sit down and say The Lord's Prayer.

It is also possible to save oneself by going into a field. One can protect oneself from the utburd by shooting, or by stabbing with a knife. But care must be taken to do everything the other way around – in other words, stab with the handle first – or else one will hurt oneself. When one stabs behind oneself in this way, there is a sound like the crying of a child or the squeaking of a pair of dry leather breeches. But when the utburd releases its hold, good care must be taken not to look back – because then one's head will remain cocked to one side for the rest of one's life.

But, as has been said, it is especially its mother the ut-burd is looking for. From Nordland, we hear that an utburd sought out its mother and tore her eyes out. And from Sweden, there is an account of a vampire-like utburd that lay down at its mother's breast and sucked her blood until she died.

It is not possible to get rid of the utburd until the body of the child has been found and placed in consecrated ground. And there is nothing the utburd would like better. Its shrieks can often be cries of distress to passersby for help in coming to rest. To a question of who it is, it replies: 'Father and mother have I none, neither was I christened nor can I lie in consecrated ground.'

The utburd is asking to be christened. It is longing for a name. If someone answers the utburd, and calls it by some chance name or other, it interprets this as a christening and settles down. For example: 'Shut up, Blabbermouth!' or 'What do you want, hairless brat?'

In this fragment of a legend from Rogaland, however, the conversation takes a somewhat different turn:

In Reindeer Gap, south of Halsarne, there was also said to have been an Utburd. There was a girl who'd had a child, but she didn't want anyone to know about it, and so she killed the child and buried it under some stones there in the Gap. Afterwards, strange cries were heard on the spot. This was probably because the dead creature was unable to come to rest, since it hadn't been given a name. But no one knew this, and people thought it was a hulder that was crying instead.

Now it happened one Sunday evening that a flock of girls went past the gap, and in the flock was the girl whose child it was. Then they heard a horrible shrieking, much louder than before. Then the mother of the child turned and shouted: 'Shut up, blabbermouth!' Straightaway a horrible laughter could be heard, and then it said, 'My mother calls me 'Blabbermouth!' The whole flock of girls heard this, and then they became suspicious. Later, the girl had to confess everything.

There are also examples of a popular christening of sorts, which was performed in order to get rid of the utburd. At Voss, a little water was taken in the hand and thrown backwards over the shoulder, so that it fell down on the utburd's head. At the same time the ceremonial words were recited. In Sogn, The Lord's Prayer was supposed to be said over a glass of spirits, which were then poured out around the person performing the christening, as he said:

> '*I christen thee at random :*
> *Guri or Jon.*'

Formulas of this kind are known from many parishes. The names Guri and Jon are reminiscent of the baptismal words in the ancient Christian decrees, in which *Jon eða Guðrun* occurs as an expression for a boy or a girl.

In Knut Strompdal's book, *Gammalt frå Helgeland*, we find this legend from Nesna:

There were children out in the forest. If someone went past the spot where they were, they began to cry. They wanted to be christened. Anyone coming across such children was supposed to take a switch, carve a cross on it and put it down in the ground. Sometimes, only a cross drawn on the ground was enough. Over this the little ones must not go. Then they were to be christened. The one to be christened stood on one side of the cross, and the one performing the christening stood on the other side. First he said The Lord's Prayer, and then he said: 'I christen thee at random – Johanna or Jon.' Then the little one was christened, and its shrieks would never be heard again.

THE DEILDEGAST

He carries glowing stones

The *deildegast* is a ghost. The word *gast* is the same as the English 'ghost', and the German 'geist'. In his lifetime, the deildegast was a stealer of land, he moved boundary stones – *deilder* – between him and his neighbor. By way of punishment, he must wander restlessly about after death. He gets no peace in the grave. Stealing land has – at all times and in every country – been regarded as one of the gravest crimes a person can commit. In the Fifth Book of Genesis (Deuteronomy 19:14) it says: 'Thou shall not move thy neighbor's landmark, which they of old time have set in thine inheritance...' And in the old Norse laws of the Gula Ting, we read that whoever moves the landmarks onto his neighbor's property, is to be regarded as a stealer of land and an outlaw.

In 'Draumkvædet' ('The Dream Song' – a visionary Norwegian ballad from the Middle Ages), we hear how people imagined that such thieves were punished after death:

> *'Then I came up to the men*
> *who carried glowing earth:*
> *Lord have mercy on those poor souls*
> *who moved deilds in the woods!'*

The deildegast is a lawbreaker who is doomed to return, again and again, to the scene of the crime. He tries to recover the landmark and move it back to where it stood. He hopes to avoid further punishment if he manages to make good the damage. But he is doomed to failure. Often he has thrown the stone in a tarn. M. B. Landstad has recorded a legend about the deildegast at Kyrdalen:

In Brunkeberg Forest there is a cottar's holding which is called Kyrdalen. Below this, and close to the highway, there is a soggy marsh, and in the marsh is a little, but deep pool. Here, Gaze Sandland has thrown a deild, thereby misappropriating a stretch of his neighbor's field. But now he must also atone for it, and, for several hundred years, he has walked there as a deildegast. During the night, he rushes up and down the boundary line, with terrible shrieks and squalls, and struggles to get the stone up again. But he never succeeds. Sometimes he manages to lift it up to the surface of the water – then a horrible laughter can be heard: Ha! Ha! Ha! Ha! But, all of a sudden, it slips out of his hands and plumps down to the bottom again. Then his wailing can be heard all over the heath: Au-hu-tu-tu! And so he must start the task anew – without rest or repose – but it always turns out the same. When he thinks he has won, it is in vain. The stone is too heavy for him, because it is weighted with his own great sin. He cannot lift it up from the deep, or undo what has already been done. For this, a greater power is needed than that of the sinful Gaze Sandland – be he a giant ten times over. Sometimes, however, he does succeed in getting the deild onto dry land, yes, even a long way up the mountain to where it has stood, but that doesn't help him at all. Because the closer he comes to the spot where the stone has stood, the heavier it grows, and all of a sudden it slips out of his hands and rolls down the mountain – the stone in front at breakneck speed, with the sparks flying, and Gaze Sandland after it, with horrible shrieks and wails. There he must toil until Doomsday.

The deildegast is doomed to a Sisyphean-labor, which will not come to a stop until Doomsday. And the gast is longing for peace. 'The stone is too heavy for me, when will Doomsday be?' he asks. Now and then it happens that people feel sorry for the deildegast and try to help him. In Telemark, according to the tradition, anyone wanting to help must meet the gast on three Thursday evenings in a row. Not until the third Thursday does the gast acquire the power of speech, and is able to tell what he has done with the deild

and where it really should stand. Then it is essential that the stone – if it has been thrown into a pond – is not lying at such a depth that the helper is unable to reach it. Often the deildegast approaches people and almost begs them for help. Then it can happen that it meets someone who does not *want* to help, and who tells him to go to Hell instead. Then, according to the tradition, the gast cries bitterly.

People tried to protect themselves against stealers of land by consecrating the stone. It was done in this way: a fire was made in the hole where the stone was to stand. Then the stone was put down in the embers, while a curse was recited – a *sigring* – which, for example, could go like this:

> *'Whoever lifts the deild so high, that the sun shines underneath – his soul shall burn in the fires of Hell.'*

There were also two witness stones – they were put down by the witnesses, one on each side of the deild. It has probably occurred to people that it is not very easy to remove ashes. It was most customary to place charcoal and birch-bark under the stones, but chalk and fragments of glass were also used. However, it happened that the thief followed the same procedure with the new, false deilds, and then, of course one was back where one had started from. The best protection was the curse. The thief had respect for this. A deild that had not been consecrated was torn up, but wherever a curse had been invoked, the thief contented himself with covering it up with earth and moss. Or else he broke off the piece of the stone that was visible. He dared not remove it.

Deildegasts often crop up after lawsuits over stretches of land and forest. No doubt it was often tempting for the loser to spread such rumors after the other party was dead. 'The landmark thief revealed himself to those he had cheated during his lifetime,' it was said.

Many public officials have had their failings mercilessly exposed, in that they were later reported to have been seen

as deildegasts. Clergymen, in particular, were often greedy
for land. Thus, a number of them became ghosts – in ruff
and gown. On the whole, it is easy to recognize a Norwegian ghost. Spooky white sheets and dancing skeletons are
virtually unknown in the tradition. Norwegian ghosts have
more or less the same appearance and the same clothes that
they had while they were alive.

Often it is related that an entire court appears, as in this
short account from Donafjell:

> In some places the deildegast has a great host with him, which
> aren't exactly pleasing to behold. They tear along, brawling and
> quarreling at the top of their lungs, some carrying bars of glowing
> steel in their hands, and some riding on black horses with fire
> spouting from their nostrils. They appear wherever the authori-
> ties and the jury, by an unjust judgement, have made themselves
> a party to the deildegast's sin, and have displaced the correct
> landmarks. Such a deildegast, accompanied by the court, walks
> up on Donafjell.
>
> Nils Grimsthveit, from Nissedal, once ran into them up there,
> while on his way back from town. He was journeying with a
> pack horse, and by the time he had come up on Donafjell,
> night had fallen and he was unable to find the path. He lost his
> way, and went a good distance into the forest. All at once, he
> heard a whole company going by – ranting and raving, bickering
> and brawling – on their way across the mountain. It seemed to
> him that he could make out officials among them. But the fire
> was spouting around them, and so he made the sign of the
> cross because he had never seen such a horrible sight before –
> and he prayed to God that he might never see it again. He was
> glad when he found the path again, and hurried as fast as he
> could to come to settled parts. – Many others have seen the
> Donafjell-gasts in the same way.

This is what happened to a court from Bø in Telemark:

> One day the mistress of Haugerud was up in the hills herding
> cattle. In the old days, there had been disputes and quarrels over
> the deilds up here, and a local inquest had once been held on the
> spot. But, rumor had it that one of the parties concerned had
> bribed a witness, so the sentence that had been pronounced had
> been a great injustice.

While she was there, she happened to gaze up at some steep slopes where the old, disputed spot of land was located, and then she saw the clerk, the bailiff and seven of the jurors going upward in single file. They were all clad in old-fashioned clothes, and were strangers to her. But from what she had heard about the men who had taken part in the hearing, she was able to tell by his bearing who each of them was. But suddenly, as she stood staring at them, they all turned into big black birds, and flew up in the air and were gone.

In more recent times, the boundary lines between the properties were more clearly defined, and the legends about the deildegast lost much of their color. As has been said above, it was believed that the gast walked in the same clothes that he had worn while he was alive. This led to the belief that the deildegast appeared in *old-fashioned* clothing: ruffled kneebreeches and a long coat, blue stockings and large shoes, and a tiny round cap on his head. In Sögne, according to legend, the deildegast was a tiny man clad in grey, with a lantern in his hand. But, from the same place, it is also reported that he had eyes as red as blood. The deildegast-legends gradually became obscure and indistinct – and were no longer of any interest. The stories were also mixed up with what had otherwise been heard about other supernatural beings. In Vestre Moland, it was said that 'the gasts were teeny weeny black men.'

As the belief in ghosts declined, many people found it difficult to tell the different beings apart. In one or two places, the deildegast was also replaced by Old Erik himself. In Gjövdal, in Aust-Agder, it was said outright that the deildegast was the devil in the shape of the person who had moved the landmark.

THE DRAUG

A headless sailor in half a boat

Out of storm and mist comes a strange vessel – half a boat. There is only one on board. He resembles a fisherman, but the clothes he wears are strangely old-fashioned – a leather hat and a long leathern jacket. Some say that his head is a tangled mass of sea wrack – others say that he has no head at all. No one who journeys on the sea wants to encounter him, because he who sails a race with the *draug* has sailed for the last time.

The word draug means 'a living dead person', an apparition. In olden times, it applied to ghosts on both land and sea, but in more recent times it is used solely in the connection *sea-draug*.

There has been a widespread belief that people who die in an unusual or unpleasant way, find no peace after death, but walk again. This is especially true of those who, for some reason or other, have not come into consecrated ground. These were thought to be dangerous to the living: they roamed about, wreaked evil upon people and tried to drag them along with them.

The draug is the ghost of someone who has been lost at sea. According to a saying of the Lapplanders from Malangen: 'He who meets with a watery grave, is tossed to and fro by the sea and turns into a draug.' The draug is nameless. He is not the ghost of someone who is known. In all likelihood, it is most accurate to regard him as a *personification* of all the dead who lie adrift in the sea.

The draug has the power to change his shape. In storms and bad weather, the fishermen encountered him in the shape that has already been described. Otherwise, it could happen that they ran into him in the guise of a seaweed-covered stone.

Evert Laukholm once came across a draug in Lofoten. Evert had been busy cleaning fish, and had been wearing mittens while working. Afterwards, he had to go down to the water to wash them. In those days, they were in the habit of taking along a paddle to beat out the dirt. Evert took the paddle, put the gloves down on a seaweed-covered stone and pounded away. When he had finished washing them, he put one of the gloves down on the stone, while he wrung the water out of the other. All at once, the stone started to roll out to sea – so fast that the water spouted up with a vengeance. That was the last he saw of both stone and mitten. A draug had been lying there.

Fishermen would not use a seaweed-covered stone as ballast in their boat, because they believed that with such a stone they might take the draug on board. And that was a sign that they would soon be shipwrecked. In Velfjord, the saying went that: 'He who takes a seaweed-covered stone as ballast in the boat, will himself lay his head on a seaweed-covered stone.' 'Laying one's head on a seaweed-covered stone' or 'getting a blade of seaweed under one's head' are ancient paraphrases for drowning.

It also happened that fishermen – especially at night, but often in calm weather – experienced the draug in a third shape: half human and half fish. The draug shrieked and pursued the boat. The story often goes that he hangs onto the sternpost and weighs the boat down, so it is on the verge of sinking. Now and then, he also manages to come up into the boat, and then good advice is worth a king's ransom...

Johan was the name of a man who lived at Kvitnes, in Velfjord. Once, when he was going to row out on the fjord, a rather strong wind started to blow which increased more and more. At the same time, the boat kept veering out of course and was so hard to row that it was practically impossible to make any headway – the boat kept heading out to sea. All at once, Johan

caught sight of a strange man sitting in the stern of the boat, and then he realized that he had the draug on board. Johan was terrified, but he was lucky enough to be able to resort to the only solution he knew – he managed to break wind. Then the draug hopped into the sea with a mighty splash of greenish-white water: he always flees from a 'working stench'. Then, when Johan went to have a look, there was a seaweed-covered stone in the ballast of the boat, and it is a well known fact that whoever takes a seaweed-covered stone into the boat, takes the draug along too.

No, in the face of a genuine 'working stench' – an *honest* fart – all evil must yield! And we can even go a step further: the draug cannot endure human excrement. A whole group of legends exists about this, usually in connection with the fact that the draug cannot leave the boats alone at night:

Whenever they journeyed somewhere, they had to make the ropes fast with all possible care: the draug was given to untying all the knots. The only certain remedy was to place human excrement on the rope they had on land. Once, when some people were out travelling, they put in at a harbor. The skipper had experienced a little of everything before, so he also knew how the draug usually behaved. And so, when he had made his boat fast on land, he went and 'did his business' right beside the rope. Later in the night, they heard a draug come up out of the sea in order to untie the hawser. But this time it did not work. 'Fie! What filth!' they heard him say up on shore. He had come up in the excrement, and it had scared him away.

As a rule, saying God's name and The Lord's Prayer also helped against the draug, but, as a matter of fact, they are not always reliable. Then it is better to use steel and fire, the traditional precautions against all kinds of spirits.

People believed that the draug could be the cause of sickness: *draugslag* ('draug-blow' – a numbness or paralysis), *draugsleik* ('draug-lick') or *draugkyss* ('draug-kiss' – a kind of sore around the mouth), *draugklyp* ('draug pinch' – a lump or swelling). Thus it was believed that the draug had come so close to the sick person that he had had an opportunity to pinch, scratch, kiss, etc.

People had special signs to go by, in order to find out whether the draug was nearby. When great quantities of jellyfish were found washed ashore in the shoals, it was believed that the draug had vomited there. Accordingly, jellyfish were called *draugspy* ('draug vomit'). In the old days, the boats were always put on land at night, either in a boatshed or under open sky. In the morning it often happened that everything on board was found topsy-turvey. If the oars were not lying the way they should, then it was believed that the draug had been up to his old tricks. The draug had tested all the seats in the boat by sitting on them. If someone lay in wait, he might just catch sight of him too. Then he would hear the draug muttering to himself: 'No, this won't do! No, this won't do!' But the draug might move to another seat, and then he could say: 'Yes, *this'll* do!' This was a sign that the man who sat there was soon going to die.

The draug always presaged something bad. It could be poor fisherman's luck, sickness, a storm, shipwreck or death. It was especially unpleasant to hear the draug shrieking from the sea. He shrieked before a storm, and whenever someone was going to die. Thus, shouts at sea were regarded as an accurate weather forecast. If people heard shouting from the sea one day, during the Lofoten fisheries, then they did not go out on the following day. The cries often came from specific places, and warned that people would be shipwrecked there. When the draug shrieked in this way, it sounded like the cries of a human being in distress. Often this was interpreted as a kind of 'echo' of cries for help from people who had been shipwrecked and drowned at that very spot. It was believed that the cries were heard every time the weather was the same as it had been when the person in question lost his life.

In Kristian Bugge's book, *Folkeminneoptegnelser*, we are told of a dramatic sea voyage. The narrator is a civil servant:

58 'In 1864, I undertook an official journey to Tromsö with a prisoner. We had an otrings boat, and in addition to myself, there were four oarsmen, the prisoner and my wife on board. When we came through Langsundet – the sound between Ringvassöy and Ressöy – in calm and lovely weather, one evening in September, we first heard the cry. It sounded quite far away, but clear.

'There's the draug,' said one of the men. 'Looks like we're going to have company through the sound.' We sat and talked about this for a little while, and all at once we heard a very disagreeable shriek which, in the stillness of the night, had a demonic effect upon us all, especially my wife. One of the boys began to mimic the shrieks, and shouted that he'd have to shriek even louder. And to tell the truth, it complied with the request to such a degree that the boy was soon struck dumb. Now it could be heard on the starboard side, now on the port side, and sometimes as if it were right underneath the boat. In the last instance, the boat shuddered and shook as if from an invisible force. Up to now, we hadn't seen anything. Then, all at once, it was as if a kind of monster shot up out of the water alongside the boat. And with a shriek, that reverberated in the surrounding mountains, the monster sank back with a long gurgling sound.

Then one of the boys took a dried coalfish that we had in the boat, and flung it at the monster, saying as he did: 'Stop your bellowing now, so we can have some peace!'

But this the boy shouldn't have done. It had been bad enough before, but now it was ten times worse. It became so disagreeable, that we found the safest thing to do was to head for land, put up the boat, and find someone who could give us a night's lodging. The people at the farm complained that the draug had been so malicious that autumn, that they hadn't been able to sleep because of the shrieking. It was worse when the moon was full. The next day, we continued on our journey to Tromsö.

On the way back, we agreed to leave the city at such an hour as to have daylight through Langsundet. But we had a strong headwind, so we made slow progress. At nightfall, my wife wanted us to moor the boat at the first farm we came to in Langsundet. But as the breeze was now light, and the current was good, I had no desire to. I wanted to come home in the course of the night. The boys agreed with me. My wife reminded us of the draug, but we replied that he would just have to try again if he liked.

No sooner had these words been uttered than we heard the first shriek. It sounded as if it came from the sea right underneath us. And the boat fairly shuddered and hopped on the water. One of the boys had had a dram, which had gone to his head, so he was out-and-out courageous and began making fun of the shrieks – offering drinks and the like. The shrieks grew wilder until it was downright terrifying and disagreeable in the darkness. My wife became frightened and wanted to head for shore, but the men turned a deaf ear to her. They took a dram at intervals, and now the wind was so good that we went at a fast clip. All at once, something hung onto the rudder and held on so tightly that we had to go back in the stern with a boathook and jab it loose. Whatever it was, we were unable to see. The shrieks became so wild and bloodcurdling that I made up my mind to put in at the first farm we came to, despite the protests of the boys. They were in high spirits – fetched from the bottle. When we came ashore, his shrieks had followed us for nearly seven miles. The boys claim that when we came up on the landing the monster was lying there. It looked like a fisherman's leathern jacket, and it dragged itself into the sea with a splash. I also heard the splash, but couldn't see a thing. In the morning, when we came to the boat and were going to continue on our way, Jens' oars were lying the other way round in the boat. He was on the verge of refusing to go into the boat with us, but came along all the same. Fourteen days later, Jens was lost at sea in a squall. The draug had claimed him.

At the bottom of this, and many other accounts, there undoubtedly lies an actual experience. Professor Svale Solheim has pointed out how well much of what has been told about the draug, can apply to the seal – especially during the rutting season in the autumn. To be sure, there is no one who believes that the *entire* tradition about the draug can arise from a single phenomenon. All kinds of experiences during the fishing have given sustenance to the tradition. But, first and foremost, we find the origins in the conceptions of the restless corpses lying in the sea. All along, the thought goes out to the drowned seaman, who is lying out there somewhere at an unknown depth – and with a seaweed-covered stone under his head.

THE SEA SERPENT

An unwelcome bathing guest

The sea serpent is a perennial visitor along Norwegian shores. We need not look any further than in the columns of the newspapers to find fresh evidence and strange reports. The belief in the sea serpent is deep-rooted and vigorous. In almost every country, and at all times, stories about sea serpents have been told. One of the oldest tales we know of is an Ethiopian legend about Alexander the Great. According to the story, an angel of the Lord showed the king a sea monster which was so long that, even though it swam very rapidly, it took all of three days to pass by the king's gaping mouth.

The oldest recorded account in Norway dates from 1555 AD: In his 'Historia septentrionalibus', Bishop Olaus Magnus wrote:

'Traders and fishermen who sail along the coast of Norway, are unanimous in their accounts of a truly remarkable story: namely, that a serpent of monstrous size – two hundred feet or more long and twenty feet wide – is to be found on rocks and in caves along the coast outside of Bergen. During the summer, when nights are light, it comes out of the caves to devour calves sheep and pigs, or else it heads out to sea to consume polyps, crabs and the like. It has hair, a yard long, hanging down from its neck, prickly scales of a blackish color, and shining, flaming eyes. It attacks the ships and carries off the people, rising in the air like a column and devouring them.'

It was mostly clergymen who wrote about the sea serpent. This does not necessarily mean that the clerical profession was especially prone to such experiences, but, quite simply,

that the ability to write was limited outside the profession.
Among the clergymen who wrote down such accounts, we
find Petter Dass, Peder Claussön Friis, Hans Ström, and
Hans Egede, the apostle of Greenland. In his book from
Greenland, 'Nye Perlustration eller Naturelhistorie' (1741),
Hans Egede tells of

'... a monstrously big marine animal which, in 1734, was
sighted off the colony at 64°, and had the following shape and
size: It was such an exceedingly large beast that its head towered
as high as the top sail of a ship, where it emerged from the water,
and its body was as big around as the ship, and at least three or
four times as long. It had a long, pointed snout, and it spouted
like a whale. It had big, broad, seal-like flippers. Its body seemed
to be overgrown with scales, and the skin was very furrowed and
rough. Otherwise, it was shaped like a serpent down below. As it
submerged, it threw itself over backwards and lifted its tail out
of the water – a whole ship's length away from its body.'

More than anyone else, the expert on sea serpents here
in Norway was Erich Pontoppidan, the Bishop of Bergen.
To be sure, he never had the pleasure of encountering the
animal himself, but he collected sworn testimonies from
far and wide, and was convinced of the monster's existence.
He arrived at the point in his studies where he even believed that he could establish the time of the sea serpent's
mating season – which he thought was in July-August.
Up to now, we have considered only those serpents which
are to be found in the sea, but they have also been sighted
in lakes. Best known, of course, is the 'Loch Ness Monster'
– or 'Nessie' as she is called by the Scots. But we need not
go all the way across the North Sea to find the fresh water
variety. The sea serpent has been observed in countless
Norwegian lakes and mountain tarns – indeed, even in
Lake Mjösa itself.
According to the tradition, these fresh-water serpents
were called 'sea serpents' because they were longing to
come to the sea. In all likelihood, the belief prevailed that

the serpents were born in lakes and deep pools, but that they moved as they grew and needed more 'Lebensraum'. There were many people who also thought that they were born on land. Pontoppidan received reports from farmers who had seen serpents, several fathoms long, in rockslides.

As they grew, the sea serpents sought out increasingly larger lakes, and when they were full-grown, the sea was the only place in which there was enough room for them. There are many accounts of the migration of the sea serpent to the sea. As a rule, it follows the rivers, but it is also capable of going shorter distances on land. Most of these accounts usually tell about a sea serpent that has somehow gotten stuck and died. At Ådal, a sea serpent came into the chute to a sawmill and plunged headlong onto the sawframe. When the flesh had rotted away, people took the sea serpent's vertibrae and used then for pillars under a stabbur. Another legend tells of a man who shot a sea serpent. The tradition also allows that a number of sea serpents have been crushed to death by floating logs.

The sea serpent was an infernal nuisance to the farmers. In the first place, it nearly frightened out of his wits everybody it came in contact with, but even worse was the fact that it stole livestock. The sea serpent sucked up the cattle that were out grazing. And if this were not enough, it could also be dangerous to *people*. Mention has already been made of the fact that it could move about on land, and from Österdal comes a legend about a boy who ran for his life in a ring around the barn – with the sea serpent snorting viciously at his heels.

But it is possible to defend oneself against the sea serpent. It has been reported, by people who have seen the sea serpent sunning itself on land, that it shone as if it were of burnished steel. But we cannot rely too much on that. From Österdal, namely, there is an account about a man at Söfinnskogen who stood fishing by a lake when he was attacked by the sea serpent. The serpent came all the way

up on land, and probably looked a bit hot-tempered, to put it mildly. But our hero found a pole and started to beat the serpent with it. And the sea serpent had to beat a hasty retreat and swim away. The man said afterwards that the serpent had been quite flabby and soft, and the pole had seemed to sink down in its flesh with each blow. Therefore, the sea serpent is not covered with steel. And in addition, according to this man, it had a mane down the length of its back.

Ivar Aasen has collected an account which tells where one can expect to find a fresh-water sea serpent: 'In a lake in which a bride has drowned, a big serpent lies twined around the bridal crown. It said that the serpent is fattening itself up on the silver.'

And now back to the coast again, because it is here that the really *big* sea serpents are to be found – and these serpents are also the most dangerous. It can often be a problem for the fishermen to keep the sea serpent at a distance, but people in Rogaland knew of a way. Torkell Mauland has described a fishing ground in Boknafjord which is called Lyrgrunnen, where no one can feel safe from the sea serpent. Whenever someone went fishing there, he would take along some dried cow dung and burn it in the boat. This usually kept the sea serpent at a distance.

Here is a legend which Mauland collected in Rogaland, in which we encounter another giant of the sea – the *seahorse :*

Once people were badly off at Hjelmeland. It had long been rumored that a sea serpent was out in the fjord, and people hardly dared go out on the water. One day a man was going to row from Rossåa to Öydeneset, and all at once he caught sight of something coming after the boat. He realized it was the sea serpent and knew it was a matter of life or death. It was clear that the sea serpent would catch up with him, and he didn't know what to do. Then he had an idea: he cut his finger and let the blood drip down on the seat. Then he put the seat down in

the water, and the sea serpent took time to lick off the blood.
Then the man had so much of a headstart that he was able to come to land. But the sea serpent kept swimming in the fjord and made it unsafe for people to go out on the water.

Later the sea serpent went to Ölesundet and blocked the way between Hjelmeland and Fister. Many people were unable to get to church, or anywhere else for that matter, even on a necessary errand. Farther up the fjord, food started getting scarce, and people were in trouble in more ways than one. Then they went to the minister and asked for advice, and the minister said they would have to hold a day of prayer in the church.

They gathered in Hjelmeland church, and the minister went up in the pulpit and started to pray. When it was over, they heard something neighing. They streamed out of the church and down to the shore, and there they caught sight of a sea horse rushing in from the sea. He came from Boknafjord and Finnfjord, and he neighed three times before he arrived. He neighed the first time as he rushed past Brakjen (off the northern tip of Finnöy), and that neigh was so loud that it could be heard over seven parishes. Then he headed through a sound to Halsnegavlen, where he neighed a second time, and then to Öydenes, where he neighed the third time.

By the time he had come to Ölesund, the sea serpent had started to flee, so the sea horse set out after it. It was a chase that was well worth watching. Umbo is the name of one of the largest islands in these parts, and Jelsa parish and Sjödnaröyane and part of Hjelmeland parish are on the same island. The sea horse chased around this island three times before he caught up with the sea serpent.

They met in Hjelmeland fjord, and here there was a battle the like of which has never been seen here in this world. It was so violent that the sea horse lost one of his hooves. But after a while he got hold of the serpent and bit it right in two.

The whole fjord was colored red with the blood. The comb and the front half of the sea serpent floated into a little inlet. The comb was later brought to Hjelmeland, where they were able to keep it for a long time. But the back half of the sea serpent remained out in the inlet and rotted, and there was such a stink that the cattle died and the trees rotted on the nearest farms, and the leaves withered on the trees as far as the eye could see. The hoof later drifted in to Hjelmeland. They took it to the parsonage and used it for a grain bin. It held forty-eight bushels of grain.

Once the battle was over, the sea horse headed out to sea again, and no one has seen him since.

At Skutesnes, on the same day, people say that three sea horses were seen offshore. After a while, two of them headed north. But the third rushed into the fjord and put an end to the sea serpent, as has been said.

THE KRAKEN

A slimy giant at the bottom of the sea

The *kraken* is a sea spirit – a sinister creature of gigantic size. It is often reported that it has tentacles like a giant squid. And it is not unlikely that it is precisely the encounter with a squid that is the background for the creation of the legend.

It is not merely a *pet* child that has many names. The kraken is also called the *krabbe* (the 'crab'), the *horv* (the 'harrow'), and the *anker-troll* (the 'anchor-troll').

It was especially on warm summer days that people encountered the kraken. In places, where the fishermen were accustomed to finding a depth of 80–100 fathoms, they suddenly measured only 20–30 fathoms. It was then believed that the sounding line had struck the kraken instead of the bottom. When lots of fish were to be had, it was a sign that the kraken was nearby, because great numbers of fish always gathered on the kraken's back.

'You must have been fishing on the kraken,' was usually said about someone who had made a good catch.

The reason why the kraken attracted so many fish, was explained in this way: during certain months the kraken eats, and then, during other months, it discharges its excrements. 'The water can be discolored from this and become somewhat thick,' writes a nineteenth century folklorist. 'This sludge is said to be so appetizing to the fish that they seek it out from every direction. And when they finally come to rest over the kraken, it opens its mouth and devours them.'

As we can see then, it is not at all safe to fish on the kraken. Tempting though it may be, it pays to get away while the going is good. As long as the kraken is attracting fish to it, it lies quietly on the bottom. Then it slowly starts rising up to the surface. And now the fisherman had better row away. As it breaks the surface of the water, it can resemble a reef – although, according to many of the accounts, we should rather say: a passably large island! A mile and a half in circumference, according to one of the legends. Thus, the kraken can be a monster the size of several kilometers, so, by comparison, even the sea serpent is an earthworm.

This 'island', or collection of reefs, is covered with something that resembles seaweed. Here and there, large humplike protuberances can be seen. The kraken is still rising up out of the sea, and finally it thrusts glistening spikes and spines up toward the sky – sometimes as high as the masts of a ship. Thereafter, it sinks abruptly. And everything in the vicinity accompanies it to the bottom in a churning whirlpool.

This interview with an old fisherman from Nordland, has been taken from Kristian Bugge's *Folkeminneoptegnelser* :

'In recent years, such strange phenomena hardly ever occur. The kraken is a sea monster which only appears during the dog days – like the sea horse and the sunfish. They only appear during really hot summers, and we haven't had any like that for the last twenty years. It was different in my childhood. That's why there were so many strange animals and fish to be seen then. I've heard many people claim that these have died out, but just let us have a flood-tide, with lots of thunder and rain, and then you'll see the multitides of strange creatures appear in the sea once more. The Lord doesn't reveal everything to us at the same time, and it's a good thing, too. If we saw all the terrible things that are at the bottom of the sea, we'd be so afraid that we wouldn't even dare come out on the water.'

'Have you ever seen the kraken yourself?'

'Yes, once. My father often told about the kraken. He came across it several times. It was especially at a fishing bank called Brosmejufta, that he saw it.

'One summer, I was rowing with Johan Kristjan out by Brosmejufta. We'd set out a longline, we'd started fishing with handlines. The fish were really biting well, but then we noticed that it was getting shallow very fast. So Johan Kristjan began to be afraid that the kraken was nearby – because it is such that lots of fish follow along with it. And if you happen to drift over it with the current, it follows slowly, and rises – almost unnoticeably – higher and higher to the surface of the water, so that you seem to be drifting toward a gently sloping reef. You can safely fish there until you reach a depth of 12 fathoms. But then you should row away quickly, preferably against the current. After a few minutes, it seems as if four poles are shooting up out of the water – as high as the mast of an otrings boat and as thick as a huge cask. Between the poles there emerges what looks like a seaweed-covered rock, and you can see the fish – the cod – pouring off on all sides. And suddenly it strikes all the poles together, so the water spouts up sky high, and the monster sinks back into the deep and takes along everything to be found within its enormous embrace.

'Well, as I said, Johan Kristjan began to be anxious about the kraken, and thought we ought to row out of its way. But we wanted to fish a while longer. We waited until we'd come to a depth of 10–11 fathoms. Then we were ordered to the oars. Our companion boat, which was lying alongside us, wouldn't listen. They felt there was no danger afoot. They waited yet another few minutes, because they were hauling in cod hand over fist.

'But then Johan Kristjan yelled over to them that they had to come – and double quick at that! They flung themselves on their oars, and when they had rowed a couple of boat lengths, all four poles thrust themselves up in the air. And they kept rising with the speed of lightning, until we could see a seaweed-covered body on the surface of the water, and fish that were rolling off on all sides. With a terrible splash, so the water spouted sky-high all around, the poles struck together, and the monster sank back with such might and speed that the undertow, with overwhelming force, dragged us all along with it. Our companion boat came into the suction, so it was on the verge of going to the bottom. But, as luck would have it, it had come so far away from the main eddies that it only danced around a couple of times, giving everyone on board the scare of his life.'

Yes, I dare say the kraken has given many a fisherman a scare. From Akershus diocese, Bishop Eric Pontoppidan has told about a couple of fishermen who stayed on the kra- ken too long:

'A couple of fishermen came over the slimy kraken with their boat. But before they were able to turn the boat, one of the kraken's spikes struck at it and managed to smash it – so they barely managed to escape with their lives in the dead calm.'

Notice that it says 'dead calm'. This is what makes the kraken so treacherous. It comes when no danger is anticipated – on a warm summer day and in calm weather.

In 1689, it was reported that a kraken had come into Ulvangen fjord, at Alstadhaug. There, its long feelers, or spikes, got caught in clefts and fissures in the rock. It was unable to free itself, and died there on the spot. According to the story, the carcass is supposed to have filled a large part of the fjord, and the stench was so bad that people could not bear to pass on that side of the fjord.

THE MERMAID

A dangerous lady of the sea

According to ancient belief, there are exact parallels in the sea to everything that has been created on land. It is this belief that lies behind strange tales about people who have seen cattle and human beings at the bottom of the sea – indeed, even managed to catch them on a hook.

Of all the marine creatures, the *mermaid* is the most celebrated. Right up to our day, artists have praised her in words and music. And the first thing we associate with the word 'mermaid' is a tiny, dainty maidenly creature – the statue of the Little Mermaid in the harbor of Copenhagen.

We are not going to shatter any more illusions than necessary, but feel obliged to suggest here and now that our modern picture of the 'hulder of the sea' is very rose-colored indeed.

Legends about mermaids have never been especially common in Norway. Their natural habitat is out by the coast, but they can also be found in rivers and lakes.

The mermaid has long hair. Like other women, she usually spends a long time combing it. Most people who have encountered her have seen her doing just that. Then she is often sitting on a stone by the water's edge. Others have caught sight of her under the boat, as she rises to the surface, and a lucky few have seen her 'walking' on the water with her hands on her hips.

The mermaid is half human, half fish – her feet have been replaced by fish's tail. In a single account she is also reported as having large breasts.

It is dangerous to come too close to the mermaid, and when she appears it is usually a sign of bad weather. But it is also said that she sings when there is a favorable wind. If someone acts contrary to her wishes, she can avenge herself in the most horrible fashion. If one sees that she is freezing – and this probably happens very often, poor thing – one should throw an article of clothing to her. Otherwise, things can turn out badly.

According to the Lapplanders, the mermaid goes into the boat in bad weather and helps steer it to land. Then one should let her take the tiller right away. There was a captain of a fishing boat in Varanger who refused to do so, and soon afterwards he lost both his sons. Thus, as likely as not, she can be a singular and sulky lady.

Bishop Olaus Magnus relates that Norwegian fishermen firmly believed that if a captive mermaid were not released again, there would be a storm. Thus, he says, it is an unwritten law that this be done. We notice a change in the relationship between the warning and what the warning is about. Originally, the mermaid, in all likelihood, merely *warned* of a storm – the sighting of a mermaid was a sign that there would soon be a storm. This has gradually been replaced by the interpretation that it is the mermaid who *causes* the storm and that the mermaid can avenge herself by sending a storm.

Andreas Faye – the first person to publish a collection of legends here in Norway – tells of a skipper who was so gruesome that he chopped off a mermaid's hand, as she placed it on the railing. Afterwards there was a disastrous storm.

The fact that the mermaid has control of winds and waves is not very strange after all. It is more extraordinary to hear that she is able to punish somebody with poverty and insanity, often unto the ninth generation.

On the other hand, the mermaid has also been heard to reward a good deed. A man from Leirfjord released a mermaid from a fish-hook, and learned in a dream where he could find a treasure. He dared not touch it, but received, nonetheless, the gift of always being safe at sea.

And this is the way the Lapplanders tell the story in one of their legends:

Two brothers went down to the shore, one moonlit night, to lie in wait for a fox that usually walked along the shore in search of fish. As they sat there, a mermaid came up out of the sea and seated herself on a stone a short distance from land. The younger brother made ready to shoot at the mermaid, but the older brother warned him and said:

'Don't shoot. It can go hard with us if you do!'

In the meantime, the mermaid sat on the stone, let down her hair and started to comb it. Again the younger brother was going to shoot, but the older brother advised against it.

'What are you thinking of? Can't you leave her alone. She's not doing us any harm, so why should you shoot at her?'

But the younger brother still paid no attention to what he said. He cocked his gun, and put the butt to his cheek. When his brother saw this, he shouted out to the mermaid:

'Beware, Mermaid, or you'll fare badly!'

At the same moment the mermaid hopped into the sea. But she came up again farther away, and shouted to the brother who had wished her well:

'If you come here at the same time tomorrow, you'll not regret it.' Then both the brothers went home. But the next evening the older brother went down alone, and seated himself in the same spot as before. He hadn't been sitting there long before a black fox came along, and this he shot. Immediately afterwards the mermaid came up out of the sea, sat down on the same stone and called to the lad to come out to her.

'You needn't be afraid,' she added, 'I won't harm you.'

The boy waded out to the mermaid.

'Now sit on my back,' said the mermaid, 'and bury your nose and mouth in my hair so you won't drown when I carry you down through the depths to my father's abode.'

The boy did as he was told. Then the mermaid dived down into the sea with him, and when they were on the bottom of the sea, she took a grapnel and gave it to him and said:

'When we come to my father's house, my father will try to find out how strong you are. But he is blind, so don't shake hands with him, but hold out the grapnel instead.'

Then they came to the spot where the mermaid dwelled.

There was no water there, nor was there any darkness. It was as light as the daylight above them, and the water stood over them like the ceiling in a loft. When the boy held out the grapnel and said, 'Good day,' the mermaid's father grasped it so hard that the claws were bent. Then they gave the boy a handsome sum of money, and to this the mermaid added a big golden beaker that had once stood on a king's table. Then they went back the same way they had come. To the boy, everything looked like glass. And the mermaid took him back to the spot from which she had taken him.

The boy became a prosperous man, and good fortune was always with him at sea. But the younger brother, who had wanted to shoot the mermaid, wasted away like a worm-eaten tree. No matter what he did, it turned out wrong. Nothing good ever came of it.

The fact that the mermaid is dangerous can also be read in the legends which have been collected among the Russian Lapplanders. Here, on the whole, she is a malicious being. She kidnaps children who make noise down by the shore, and she takes a strangle-hold on people who go swimming, causing them to drown.

In Sparbu it was said that if the mermaid sang, the fishing would be good. According to the lore of the Lapplanders from Utsjok, she drives the fish up into the rivers so there will be a good catch.

The mermaid also has a certain connection with the fodder. From Hedmark we hear that the mermaid usually comes ashore with her cows at Michaelmas. If a southerly wind is blowing on that day, it is a bad omen because then the fodder will be consumed too quickly. In Sparbu, if there was a southerly wind on Michaelmas Day, the barn doors were barred to keep the mermaid from coming with her oxen and eating up the fodder. At Helgeland, an axe was placed in the haymow on Christmas Eve to keep the 'Sea Troll' from coming and eating up the fodder from the cattle. People were also supposed to sweep up carefully around the chopping block, because the mermaid came and danced around it on Christmas night.

The mermaid is an intelligent lady. In Vågå it is said outright that, 'The mermaid is supposed to know everything.' People who encounter her often take the opportunity of questioning her about various things. Then she always gives an oracular reply. There are many legends about this.

Legends about erotic relationships between mermaids and young men have been popular material for the storytellers, as well might be expected. However, these stories are often hard to distinguish from folktales, and familiar, well-worn folktale motifs are woven into the plot.

THE MARE

An unwanted bedfellow

The belief in the *mare* is widespread throughout Europe, and we have examples from both the Middle Ages and Antiquity. As a rule, the mare is thought of as a female, demon-like being which delights in tormenting people at night. Most often she concentrates her attentions on men. The mare can change her shape, and make herself so tiny that she can crawl in through the keyhole. Indeed, even the tiniest crack is big enough for her. Like a vapor she steals in. When she has come into the bedroom, she goes over to the bed and mounts the sleeper's chest so he has difficulty in breathing and, accordingly, bad dreams. A bad dream is usually called a 'nightmare'. This is not correct. The bad dream is *caused* by the nightmare – by the fact that the mare is sitting astride the sleeper.

As a rule, the mare has human shape – very often she *is* a human being. An inner urge can compel her to roam about at night as a mare. During the day it is difficult to tell by looking at her. Perhaps she does not even remember it herself.

Who becomes a mare? If a mother has seven daughters, one of them will be a mare. And even more certain: if, in a supernatural way, a woman manages to free herself from labor pains – for example, by wearing a wolfskin girdle, by crawling through the skin of a foal or the after-birth of a mare – and she then gives birth to a daughter, the daughter is doomed to be a 'mare'. It is also supposed to be possible to identify ladies with a craving for such nocturnal escapades. It is said that the mare has eyebrows that meet, and she has no hair under her arms!

Mares are most often thought of as young maidens. They can also be pretty, we hear. Thus, it is somewhat disconcerting to discover that a branch of the tradition allows for mares that are old, unmarried women who walk. At Ål, in Hallingdal, she was described as 'a shrew'. The mare is usually thought of as a *female* spirit, but there are examples of the mare being of the male sex. It stands to reason that women are haunted most by *such* mares. Thus, the erotic motive should be fairly obvious. In Lista, the mare was regarded outright as a personification of romantic yearnings. It was said that if a man acquired a mare, there was a woman who desired him, and if a woman were visited by a mare, there was a man who desired her.

In Sigdal and Eggedal, the mare – or *muru*, as it was called – had the shape of a cat. This was supposed to be a person who was sexually abnormal. The cat – the *marekatt* ('the mare cat') – is a motif that recurs in many parts of the country, and the cat, of course, is a *black* cat.

The mare can also appear in the shape of a ball of yarn – a not uncommon form of shapeshifting among the hidden people. The connection with the hidden people is also apparent from the fact that many people believed that the mare had been *sent* by the hidden people. But in Odda they had arrived at a different conclusion: Mares were ghosts that hovered in the sky.

The mare was a nuisance – not only to people, but to animals as well. She can ride the horses in the stall, until they are found the next morning drenched with sweat. But not only is she a nuisance, she can also be downright dangerous. Among other things, one should take good care not to sleep with one's mouth open. According to reliable sources throughout the country, if the mare manages to count all the teeth in the sleeper's mouth, then he or she must die!

How then was it possible to protect oneself against this sinister creature? It was supposed to help to put down one's shoes in such a way that the toes were turned away from the bed. It was believed, namely, that the mare had to step into them before she climbed up in the bed, and she would be unable to manage it if the shoes were facing the wrong way! Placing ones shoes in reverse order could also help, i. e. putting the left shoe to the right of the other. A horseshoe over the door was supposed to be effective – especially if all the nails had been left in it. A double cross could also be painted on the door to the bedroom. Then the mare was unable to come in that way, at any rate. Many people also took comfort in having something made of iron – preferably steel, of course – under their beds, or a pair of scissors or a knife under their pillows. Steel helps against mares as well as other ghosts. There were also a number of people who said a special evening prayer as protection against the mare. One of these prayers goes like this:

> *'Mare, mare so tiny!*
> *Mare, mare so tiny!*
> *Here's a lever, here's a spear!*
> *Out you'll run if you're in here!*
> *Here's powder, here's a gun!*
> *If you're in here, out you'll run!'*

A similar formula is to be found in an account from the Faroe Islands. Here we are told how to find out whether the mare is inside the house or not:

'In the evening she may very well be inside, even if one cannot see her. It is possible to find out by placing a knife in the centre of a kerchief or a garter, folding the two sides together – one on top of the other – and rolling it up with the knife inside. Then it is passed around the waist three times, while one recites:

> *'Mare, mare so tiny,*
> *if you're inside,*
> *don't you remember the blow*
> *that Sjurdur Sigmundarson once*
> *gave you on the nose?*
> *Mare, mare so tiny,*
> *if you're inside*

out you'll go
bearing both stones and turf
and everything in here!'

If the knife has worked itself loose, when the kerchief is unfolded, the mare is not inside. But if, on the other hand, the knife is still lying where it was placed, then the mare is inside the house, and the ritual must be repeated three times in order to drive her out.'

Lighted candles were also supposed to keep the mare at a distance. At Hvaler, a sheath-knife was placed in the wall over the bed. If the mare still came, one was supposed to swing the knife three times over one's head while saying: 'In the name of Jesus.' Here too they had another, somewhat more unconventional method:

'It was possible to save oneself from the mare by throwing one's petticoat at it. A woman was helping out in a house. She was pestered by the mare in that house. When the marecat came back, she flung her green petticoat at it, and it started to claw and tear at it. In the morning she saw, to her horror, that the mistress of the house had green threads between her teeth.'

As a curiosity, mention can also be made of the fact that when little boys in Verdal went about whistling through their fingers, the old folks used to say: 'You shouldn't whistle through your fingers, because then you'll get visitors tonight.' Whistling through one's fingers was the same as summoning the mare.

When it came to protecting their livestock, people were also uncommonly resourceful. Hanging a scythe or some other sharp object in front of the stable was supposed to help. A dead magpie could also be used. In many places, people also hung up a *murukvist* (mare-sprig) over the barn and stall doors. On spruce and fir trees one may find a tiny swelling out of which a number of tiny twigs are growing. This is what is called a *murukvist*. Many people kept such sprigs on hand for any eventuality. In other places, a matted tuft of tiny twigs from a birch tree was also used for the same purpose. This was called 'Simon's Scourge'. At Röm-

6 – Phantoms.

skog, in Östfold, a *marelokk* (mare-lock) was used. This is a stunted branch, usually of spruce, with a luxuriant growth of tiny needles. Whenever someone wanted to bring home such a marelokk, he had to be careful not to carry it across a road along which a dead body had just been driven. Otherwise the marelokk would lose its powers. At Römskog, a broomstick could also be placed by the barn or stall door. Then the mare dared not go in. The broomstick also served the same purpose as the marelokk.

If a cow were tormented by the mare while she was standing in the barn during the winter, it could also help to hang a bell on her. If the mare rides a cow, the milk can turn bad and sour.

All things considered, it seems unlikely that anyone would dare to *marry* a mare, but, as a matter of fact, one man did. Sophus Bugge recorded this legend from Kviteseid in Telemark:

There was a man who was ridden by a mare every night. He could not tell where the mare came in, but then he saw a hole in the wall and there he pounded in a cock. When he went to have a look in the morning, there was a naked woman crawling about on the floor. He bought clothes for her and dressed her up. She was as pretty as could be, so he had her christened and married her. They lived together for eight years and had five or six children.

But one Christmas Eve the man was quite drunk, and then he asked her about her kinfolk. She said that she had not known her father or her mother.

'Well, I don't know where you came from,' he replied, 'but now I'll show you where you came in.' And then he took out the cock. At the same moment she popped out through the hole, and he never saw her again.

When a legend tells of a marriage between a mare and a young man, this is very likely a feature that has been borrowed from other tales about marriages between mortals and supernatural beings. The origin is most likely to be found in the folktale about the Swan-maiden.

THE WEREWOLF
At the full of the moon

Werewolf – the name is derived from the Old English *wer* (man) and *wulf* (wolf), and literally means 'a man-wolf'. In all likelihood, it has its direct background in hunting magic, and in the jerkin of animal skins that many warriors used in the really hard, old days. It was often believed that, in this way, one assumed some of the characteristics of the beasts of prey; one identified oneself with and imitated the animal. Clad in the skin of a wolf, and with the wolf's head for a hood, the warrior stormed forth, growling at the enemy. No wonder that the opponents were willing to swear, afterwards, that it really *was* a wolf they had been fighting against.

The belief that a human being can transform himself into a beast of prey is well known, so to speak, throughout the world. In the North, and in the rest of Europe, it is usually a question of wolves or bears.

When someone wanted to change his shape, he usually buckled on a girdle of wolfskin. The part represented the whole, and immediately he was clad in the complete skin of a wolf. He regained his normal shape by taking off the girdle. The use of witches' ointments and magic formulas, in order to achieve the desired result, was also customary. In Germany, however, it was believed – for reasons unknown – that a girdle made from the skin of a hanged man was just as effective as a girdle made from the skin of a wolf. Whoever transforms himself in this way, assumes not only the shape of the wolf, but the nature of the wolf as well. He becomes a constant danger to the livestock of others. And worst of all: with the transformation follows a voracious appetite for human flesh. It is a common European belief that werewolves go hunting especially at night – at the full of the moon – and often in packs.

As late as the 16th and 17th centuries, veritable witch-hunts were organized for werewolves, and those who were captured were mercilessly sentenced to the pyre. In early court documents, we are able to follow several such 'werewolf-trials'. In 1590, a man from Bedburg, near Cologne, was sentenced to death as a werewolf. He was found guilty of having killed – as a werewolf – thirteen children and two pregnant women, and of being in the habit of transforming himself into a wolf with the help of a magic girdle. In the court documents it says that, when they pursued him and finally surrounded him, they saw him let the girdle drop to the ground – and immediately he was standing there in human shape.

This business about the *girdle* does not always have to be included. According to a number of accounts, the one who wants to transform himself, crawls into the complete skin of a wolf. During the night he is a werewolf, but at daybreak he takes off the wolfskin and hides it. There is a remarkably intimate connection between the skin and its owner. If the wolfskin is hidden in a cold place, the owner goes about with his teeth chattering the whole day. If it is found by someone else and destroyed, the owner dies.

The werewolf tradition is far from homogeneous. As a rule, two widely different types of 'man-wolves' are allowed for. First and foremost, there is the one *wants* to be a werewolf, and who, by the use of magic aids, *periodically* appears in a wolfskin. Then we have the person who has been bewitched by others. Someone – as a rule a Finn or a Lapplander – has cast a spell over him, and he is domed to live for years as an animal.

In Selbu, many tales were told about a Finn named Andrianus, who was well-versed in the art of magic:

Once he changed a rich man into a wolf – a miserly fellow, who could never afford anything, but only went in for stealing what he could from others. Then it happened, because of a deal, that Andrianus was angry with him too, and so he changed him into a wolf. According to the story, the rich man remained a wolf for three years, and then he was able to feel what it was like to go hungry. But afterwards, when he had turned into a man again, he would cry every time he heard the wolves howling. 'No one can imagine how much the wolf starves,' he said, and then he hastened to turn out a cow for them. Every Christmas Eve he was in the barn, and let out his big ox to them . . .' 'so they won't have to starve tonight, at any rate,' he said.

During the war with Russia, in 1808–09, people in Sweden believed that the Russians transformed Swedish prisoners into werewolves, and sent them home to harass the land. Such 'bewitched' werewolves usually attack pregnant women in order to get hold of the fetus. It is said, namely, that if the werewolf succeeds in drinking fetal blood, the spell is broken and he becomes a human being forever.

In addition to these two types of werewolves, we must take into account yet another variant – in the Norwegian tradition, at any rate. We have many accounts of people who, periodically, turn into werewolves against their will, and, apparently, without anyone casting a spell on them. Long periods can elapse between each time. The story is told about a man from Östfold, who assumed the shape of a wolf for seven or eight days each summer. Then he vanished into the forest. When he came back – emaciated and exhausted – he was unable to give an account of where he had been. From Romsdal, there is the story of 'Greylegs Arne'. He too was an innocent, periodic werewolf. His story is told in the truest 'Dr. Jekyll and Mr. Hyde' style:

One day, when Arne and the hired girl were in the hay field together, he felt the spell coming over him. And so he warned the girl that she must flee up in a tree. And she was hardly up in the tree when Arne dropped the scythe and his clothes, popped into a wolfskin, started howling like a wolf and vanished into the forest.

Before long, he came back in human shape, put his clothes on and started mowing again. But it was high time she'd come up in the tree, he said to the girl – because when his periods as a wolf came over him, he couldn't keep from tearing to pieces every living thing within reach.

After such periods as a wolf, he was pale and weak, so in all likelihood it was a hardship on him. Otherwise, he was kind and easy to get along with.

Let us return to the original werewolf – the evil 'man-wolf'. Against one of these, ordinary lead bullets did not help. During the casting, it was either necessary to have a barleycorn in the bullet, or else – and this was even better – one could shoot with a silver bullet. It was quite customary to use a silver collar stud for this purpose. A Black Book recommends, in addition, that during the casting of the bullet the lead be mixed with the heart and liver of a bat.

As has been said above, the werewolf was especially dangerous to pregnant women. But there was one remedy that kept him away: namely, grey stones. If the possible victim had grey stones inside her shirt, then she could feel comparatively safe. In Idd, people used to say: 'A woman who is with child must always carry grey stones on her body, or else the werewolf will get her!' It was also possible to save oneself by calling the werewolf by name – guessing who it was. A man in Idd once caught sight of two werewolves who were about to attack his wife. He thought he recognized them, and so he shouted as loudly as he could: 'Ola and Per, don't do that!' And immediately the skins dropped off them, and Ola and Per took to their heels as fast as they could. It is also a consolation to know that, if the pregnant woman is carrying a boy, and the boy in the mother's womb has already gotten two teeth in his mouth, then the werewolf can do her no harm.

As we have already seen, it is possible to become a werewolf quite involuntarily. At Hvaler, it was said that, 'If the parents are unfaithful during their marriage, their boys will turn into werewolves and the girls into mares.' Or perhaps the mother had used a wolfskin girdle during the birth? According to a central European belief, the wearing of such a girdle was supposed to make the birth easier, but the children were doomed to be werewolves.

Many people believed that it was possible to tell by *looking* at a man whether he was a werewolf or not. If his eyebrows met, it was a suspicious sign. Such eyebrows were 'werewolf-brows' pure and simple. And, in addition, if the suspect was so unfortunate as to have a growth of hair between his shoulder blades, then it was an open – and – shut case.

People were not very interested in what became of the werewolves after they died. But, in all likelihood, it was assumed that they had sold themselves to the Devil. As a matter of curiosity, however, it should be mentioned that, according to the ancient Greeks, a man who in this life had been a werewolf, would turn into a vampire when he died...

THE GARDVORD

A supernatural caretaker

The *gardvord* is a spirit that safeguards the farm, the people who live there and their domestic animals. The tradition about him is quite obscure, and is mixed up with the conception of another household spirit – the *nisse*, also known under the name of *tusse*, *tuftebonde*, *tuftekall*, *tomte* and *gobonde*. Or perhaps it is more correct to say that the nisse is the gardvord under a new name and a somewhat altered character.

The tradition about the gardvord is best preserved in Vestlandet. Here he also goes under the name of *gardsbonde*, *tunvord* and *tunkall*. The gardvord must originally have been thought of as a ghost of one or more of the ancestors of the farm. As a rule, people were afraid of ghosts. These were human beings who had something left undone or unavenged – and a cold air blew off them. But the gardvord was not feared. He was welcome. The conceptions about him were bound up with happiness and prosperity on the farm. Perhaps it was the *rudkall* himself – the one who had cleared the land and built the farm – who walked.

The gardvord kept all evil powers away from the farm. Even the *oskorei* gave it a wide berth if the gardvord lived there.

In Barbro's barn, there was no end of demons. But as soon as she marked the cows with crosses on their backs, the peaked-cap nisses and tusses and troll cats flew over in the corners and hid. – Now the gardvord was quite a different and better sort, he was. If he got his fill on Christmas Eve, he faithfully kept watch over house and farm. – He stayed in an old oak above the yard.

It was hollow and could hold four or five men. Every Christmas Eve, the farmer's wife cooked tasty cream porridge and baked good oatcakes, and put them inside the oak. By morning, he had eaten up every last bit.

Like so many other fantastic figures of popular belief, the gardvord had the power to change his shape. He could make himself as tiny as he liked. But usually – according to an account from Hardanger – he was so big that, when he stood between two houses, he could rest both arms on the roofs.

The crux of the tradition about the gardvord are the conceptions of the way he *dwelled* at the farm, because it was a matter of course that this supernatural caretaker also had to have his night's lodging there. This gardvord-bed has been amply described in the tradition, but opinions differ as to where it was and how it looked. Many have described it as a *lair* – a pallet as for a dog or a cat – and relegated it to the barn. If anyone else tries to lie down there, he is thrown out by invisible hands. The fact that the bed resembles the sleeping place of a dog or cat indicates that people have probably thought of the gardvord as a spirit in the shape of an animal. But this must obviously be a digression in the tradition. And the relegation to the barn is most likely the result of an influencing from the tradition about the nisse. Characteristic of *this* spirit is the fact that he hangs out in the stable and the stall, and that he usually dwells in the barn. It is here, as we know, that he sits with his Christmas porridge.

It was generally believed that the gardvord had the shape of a human being, and that he lay in a bed that was reserved for him alone. The bed always had to be made, and no one else was allowed to use it. The bed stood in the *bu* or the *loft*. These must not be interpreted as rooms in the farmhouse itself: they were separate buildings that belonged on the old farms. Th. S. Haukenæs has described them as follows:

'In the old days, they had a separate building on the farm which they called the 'loft'. It was a house, two stories high, that stood on pillars of wood or stone as protection against rats and mice and the like. The bottom storey was called the 'bu', and the children and the servants had their sleeping quarters here. Some people also used the building for a *stabbur* (storehouse), and let the household sleep in the cowshed or the stall. Around the stabbur, or bu, ran a wooden gallery two or three alens wide, with upright posts along the outside. The second storey, then, was the 'loft' itself. It was so big that it extended out over both the stabbur and the gallery underneath. The loft was the 'finery-house' of the farm. It was here they kept their Sunday finery, and all the new bedclothes which hung on long poles under the beams; and it was here they had all their rose-painted chests – one for each member of the family, from the youngest to the oldest – and it was here they had sleeping accomodations for strangers and guests. This method of building is supposed to have been in fashion from the period before the Black Death.'

The fact that the gardvord had his bed here, indicates that he was an *honored* guest, and that he was respected more highly than most guests – since he was supposed to have a bed of his own in which no one else was permitted to sleep. Again and again the legends tell of people who tried to lie down in the gardvord-bed, and of how badly they fared. The purpose of these tales has undoubtedly been to imprint upon the younger generation a respect for the gard-vord, and, with that, for other ancient customs and traditions as well.

Thus, the gardvord's bed was a permanent fixture in certain types of buildings: the *loft* or the *bu*. But today these houses are gone. They belonged to the ancient farm society, in which every occupation on the farm had its own building, assembled around a common yard. Loft and bu were torn down, when the neighbors moved away from the old yard and put up new houses separately. And, accordingly, the very conception of, and the legends about, the gardvord lost the conditions of their existence. The peasant society entered into a new phase. And many of the ancient beliefs

were discarded because they stood in the way of progress.
A marked change in the attitude to the gardvord is also apparent. From being an ancestor, who brought happiness and prosperity to his descendants, he became an evil power, who hindered all progress and who, therefore, had to be destroyed. It became customary to tell stories about courageous men who dared stand up to the gardvord, throw him out of the bed and send him packing from the farm:

At Tengesdal, in Hylsfjord, there was a tunkall who stayed in the bu. When strangers came to the farm, and were supposed to sleep in the bu, they were usually thrown out on the floor as soon as they had gone to bed. The man of the farm was called Njædl. He was an unusually strong fellow, and preferred to be master of his own house. One day he made up his mind to go to bed in the bu. No sooner had he lain down than the tunkall grabbed hold of him and was going to throw him out. But Njædl put up a struggle. He took his knife, and slashed and stabbed and jabbed on all sides – hacked at the walls and carried on something terrible. Then the tunkall became frightened. He ran to the pigsty and hid. Njædl set out after him, he didn't want the fellow there either. He didn't stop until he had chased the tunkall away from the farm. When he had come a little way down the hill, the tunkall looked back and cried. All over the farm, they could hear him sobbing until he was gasping for breath.

The gardvord became an evil spirit, against which people had to protect themselves. Some even maintained that he was prone to stealing. And there are examples of people tying ribbons around the necks of their livestock in order to *protect* them from the gardvord. Thus, the whole of the ancient tradition about the gardvord began to disintegrate. The gardvord borrowed traits from other evil creatures, and in the end became synonymous with the Evil One himself – a devil who had to be conjured away by 'Black Book Parsons', experts at the task. And with that, we have come to the end of the belief in the gardvord.

On his travels, the devil spends the night at the farms – sometimes here and sometimes there. Thus, at each farm, they had to have a bed which stood ready to receive him. Christian people must never lie in it, because it was the bed of the devil – or gardvord, as he was called by some.

Such a bed stood at Lutro. – Late one dark autumn evening, the parson came to the farm and asked for a night's lodging. Then they were in a bad fix – they had only *one* empty bed, and no one dared lie in that because it was the bed of the Evil One or gardvord, they said.

'Oh indeed, in that bed I'd like to lie,' said the parson, and asked where it stood. Oh, it stood in the loft, where it had been from time immemorial. But if the parson valued his life, then he mustn't go there.

'Oh yes, that's exactly where I want to lie,' he said, and then he went up to the big loft and went to bed. No sooner had he come under the rug than he was thrown out so forcibly that it seemed as if every bone in his body would break. He scrambled up in the bed again, but made the same journey once more. He crawled up in the bed this time too, and thought that the nasty creature would soon have to give up. But before he could catch his breath, he was taken by the arms and feet and flung like a rag way across the floor. Now he thought it was time to put an end to the game. He took out his Black Book, and conjured the Devil fast to the floor. Then he went down to the farmer and asked for a candle. When he came back and made a light in the room, a grey-clad fellow was standing on the floor. He had the horns of a billygoat, and on one foot he had a cloven hoof, and he had claws on his fingers. He was so hopping mad that fire and brimstone were pouring from his mouth. But the parson didn't hesitate. He took out a pin, and pierced a hole through the leaden frame around the glass. Now the Evil One changed his tune. He pleaded very meekly to be allowed to go out through an auger hole in the wall. But the parson insisted, and through the leaden frame he had to go – even though it proceeded with both toiling and moiling and whimpering and whining. Then the parson went down to the farmer and said that, from now on, he could let anyone use the bed in the loft who wanted to.

THE NISSE

A helpful ally – a dangerous foe

The *nisse* is a spirit that lives on the farm and helps the farmer with the work. He is thought of as a tiny fellow clad in grey, with a grey or white beard, and a little red cap on his head. He is not exactly a beauty. 'Ugly as sin,' they said in Østerdal. He has a big, thick, protruding lower lip. His eyes glitter, and his whole body is covered with hair. He has no thumbs. He often resembles a little round ball of yarn. In Numedal, it was said that he was so tiny that he had trouble crossing the threshold. And in the little valleys around Lindesnes, they tell of a married couple who – when they were going to move – took the nisse with them in a little kit, which the wife carried in her hand. But, as a rule, he was probably thought of as being the size of a dwarf. The nisse is related to the *hidden people*. In Idd, it was thought that the nisses were the fallen angels that are referred to in the Bible.

The body of a nisse has been found:

On Brattöa, an island near Halden, a dead nisse was found many years ago. And then, of course, there was a chance of seeing just what kind of a strange creature this was. On closer inspection, it turned out that the nisse was a kind of animal with a red comb – almost like a cock's comb. The story goes that people from Hvaler went out to Brattöa in a body to have a look at him. 'He was jellylike, and so heavy that they had to bury him where he lay,' they said. It was believed that lightning had put an end to him.

The name 'nisse' is not very old in Norway, but the personage himself is well known. If anything, the nisse must be regarded as a later replacement of more ancient phenomena. In many respects he has taken over the functions of the gardvord. The name 'nisse' occurs, for the most part, in the rolling countryside of Östlandet, in the cities and, to a lesser extent, in the Agder districts. Elsewhere the name is rare, and in the typical nisse legends, other spirits crop up. It is the hidden people, or the haugbonde, who look after the house and farm.

The nisse keeps to the stall and the barn, and it is particularly the animals that benefit from his work. On farms where there is a nisse, the animals are always full and well-groomed. He is especially fond of horses. In Idd, they say that he likes grey and black horses the best. He usually picks out a favorite horse, and this one receives better care than the others. He likes to plait the horses' manes. Such plaits are called *nisse-* or *tusse-plaits*, and it can be dangerous to try to undo them. One must consider oneself fortunate if one gets off with a pain in one's fingers.

The nisse does not tolerate having the horses he likes mistreated or sold. It has happened that he has accompanied his favorite horse to its new owner. And a wife, who does not take care of the cows the way she should, risks nightly visits and a thrashing at her bedside! A hired girl, who did not take hold of a newborn calf gently enough, was beaten by the nisse until she was crippled.

The nisse steals grain and hay, and carries it home to the farm where he lives. During such nightly raids, it happens that he encounters other nisses on the same errand. Perhaps they have even dared to steal from the farm where he lives himself! Then they fight tooth and nail.

A few people have tried to excuse the nisse, and maintain that he steals from the rich and gives to the poor. But this hardly holds water. The nisse is an incurable thief. Where the nisse lives, flour bins – in loft and bu – are never empty.

And one should never underestimate the amount of what he hauls to the farm in this way:

There was a man in Hjartdal who had the strangest good fortune with his cattle, and no matter how many cows he held, he was always well supplied with fodder. His haymow lasted such a long time that it never seemed to come to an end. Now it happened one night that the man was sleeping out in the barn, when along came a little nisse dragging a couple of straws of hay. He panted and struggled, and seemed to be having quite a lot of work with his heavy burden. The man thought this was ridiculous, and said in a mocking voice: 'Well, that was something to be dragging so heavily.' Then the nisse became angry and said that now he was going to drag as much *from* him as he had dragged *to* him before. Then he would see if it was worth mocking at. And it didn't take long before the man's fodder was used up and his cattle had starved to death. Nothing succeeded for him and he became a poor man.

Otherwise, the nisse usually takes part in honest work too. It has happened that he has done the day's work of a grown man, before the farm hands have managed to get out of bed.

The nisse lives alone, and has neither wife nor children. 'All the same, he's always in good spirits, merry and contented,' said people in Lindesnes, 'as long as he's allowed to go about his business in peace, and receives his food like everyone else on the farm.'

The nisse costs little to feed. He is supposed to have food every Thursday evening; often, only one meal a year will do – on Christmas Eve. But in return, it is supposed to be a real feast: a big portion of cream porridge, and, as a rule, an abundance of ale. And n.b! *There is supposed to be a lump of butter in the porridge.* The food is placed in the barn or in the stall. (In Denmark, it happened that they put it on the roof of the stall!)

It has been mentioned that the nisse is a merry fellow, but he is also quick to fly into a rage. And he is never angrier than when someone has forgotten to put the lump of butter in his porridge. The story goes that, in order to play a trick on the nisse, a hired girl hid the butter at the bottom of the plate. When the nisse did not find the butter right away, he became so angry that he went right down to the barn and killed a cow. Then he began to eat the porridge. But at the bottom, of course, he found the butter. The nisse repented. Then he hit upon a remedy. In the course of the night, he dragged the dead cow over to the neighboring farm, stole a cow and put the dead cow in its place.

It has also happened that the girl, who was supposed to put the porridge out in the barn, has eaten it up herself. By way of punishment, the nisse has grabbed hold of her and forced her to dance with him. Faster and faster, wilder and wilder – until she was foaming at the mouth and nose. 'If the Nisse's porridge you did eat, the Nisse will dance you off your feet!' sang the nisse.

Two strangers once came to a farm at nighttime. They were hungry, but did not want to wake up the people of the farm. They went into the barn. There they found the nisse's food. They ate it before they continued on their way. When the nisse came and found the dish empty, he gave a snort so the whole barn shook, set fire to the outhouses and went away.

At a farm in Kvinesdal, the nisse received little and bad food. In the end, he flew into a rage. He took the stabbur on his back(!) and carried it a long way up the hillside. But it was too heavy. He sank to his knees and exclaimed irritably: 'Buttermilk and burnt bread bring a man down on his knees!'

A Danish legend can also testify to the fact that the nisse – in spite of his size – has such gigantic strength: A hired boy once saw a nisse sitting out in the yard, picking lice out of his shirt. A cloud came in front of the moon, and the nisse said: 'Shine, big man Moon so I can see to crack my lice!' The boy sneaked up behind the nisse, and struck him over the back with a stick. The nisse turned in a flash, and threw the boy high above the rooftop. The first two times he caught him, but the third time he let him fall to the ground, so he was killed.

But the nisse is also something of a prankster, and is quite fond of playing tricks on people. In the darkness, he often lies in the way of people, making them stumble. He is also blamed for letting out the cows, tweaking the cat by the tail, blowing out the candle and kissing the dairymaid(!)

He can make an infernal racket in the kitchen, as if cups and glasses are being broken. But when people come running, they find everything intact. Then the nisse laughs.

But the nisse can also find time for more innocent fun. Here in Norway – especially on moonlit nights – nisses can often be seen toboganning or racing over the fences. Now and then, the nisse mingles with the children when they go sliding on the barn bridge. Then he usually slides on a chip, and he goes just as well uphill as downhill. A man from Hvaler is supposed to have seen the nisse go iceskating.

The nisse is a faithful and loyal farmhand. He stands by his master through thick and thin. But often this can make him do quite drastic things. Thus, a nisse is once said to have gone right through the wall of the barn belonging to one of his master's enemies, and to have broken the leg of a cow.

Now and then the nisse can be regarded as a personal *vord* – a guardian 'angel' that follows his master wherever he goes. He is invisible to most people, but a few can see him. This too can produce an undesirable result. The story goes that several Norwegian farmers were so downright fed up with their nisse, that they did everything possible to get away from him. But even though they moved from the farm, it did not help. The nisse moved too, and followed them faithfully like a shadow.

The nisse wants peace and quiet in the evening. He does not like to hear pounding or loud voices in the house late at night. He himself gets up at the crack of dawn, and he needs sleep. He expects the people of the farm to follow his example: early to bed and early to rise. If they make noise all the same, he unties the cows and chases them out of the barn.

The fact that the nisse takes revenge, whenever there is no peace at night, has been mixed up with the belief in ghosts. From Konsmo, there is a story about a nisse who pestered the people of the farm every night. When they had gone to bed, he went up and down the stairs and dragged iron chains after him.

In many places, the story goes that the nisse cannot stand swearing. Anyone who swears, receives a box on the ear from the nisse.

Where the nisse lives, people are safe from fires. But, if the nisse moves, you can just as well move yourself, because then an accident is imminent. On board many of the fishing boats along the coast, there used to be ship's nisses in the old days. As long as they are on board, one can be safe, but if they abandon the boat, it is an omen of shipwreck.

The nisse draws wages for the work he does on a farm. He takes a third of every crop, but when and where the division takes place, no one knows or notices.

From Tjölling, there is a legend about someone who wanted to please the nisse by giving him new clothes as payment for good work:

On a farm – it was somewhere in Jarlsberg, I think – they had a nisse who was very kind and helpful. But he could get angry too, and then he wasn't easy to get along with. Then he would do things like putting the newborn calves down in the bucket, pouring out the milk for the dairymaid and many other pranks. Therefore, both the farmer and the dairymaid thought it best to please the nisse in everything within reason, and they certainly didn't regret it either. The dairymaid took great care to put out really fine cream porridge in the barn every holiday, and on Christmas Eve she put an extra big lump of butter in it, so the porridge would be rich and good. And, at Christmas time, the farmer didn't forget to put out new clothes for the nisse, so he wouldn't freeze in the wintry cold.

It was easy to see that the nisse appreciated all the good things he got, for nowhere did the cows thrive so well as on that farm. Not to mention the horses! For the nisse took a particular fancy to them. When the farmer came home, he didn't even have to put the horses in. He just unharnessed them and the nisse took care of the rest – put them in the stable, rubbed them down with a wisp of straw, took down hay to them and filled the bucket with water. The farmer knew this, and so he let the nisse take care of the horses the way he liked. And, as he was so well pleased with the nisse in every way, he put out a fine pair of white leather breeches for him one day.

The next day the man and the boy had been out driving, and, as it was raining as though the heavens had opened, they left the horses standing outside and hurried in the house. They thought the nisse would put them in the way he usually did. But the one who didn't come, that was the nisse. They had gone over to the window, to see how the horses were getting along, and there stood the nisse, quite content, in the door of the stable, with his hands deep in the pockets of his new leather breeches.

The man became annoyed, as you can imagine, and so he went to the door and shouted: 'My good nisse, what does this mean? Don't you see the horses today?'

But then the nisse slapped his thighs with both hands, and laughed so hard that he almost fell over. When he had finally caught his breath, he straightened up, stuck out one leg, thrust his hands down in his pockets again and said, 'Well, you certainly don't expect me to go out in this nasty weather with my new, white leather breeches on, do you?'

In the eyes of the Church, the nisse was also a demon and a helper of Satan – Indeed, he was often identified with the Evil One himself.

In Denmark, it was said that the nisse never ate the butter he received in his porridge. He hid the butter, because in it he was going to fry the souls of everyone he had been connected with here on earth.

In Sweden, they said that the nisse is entitled to one joint of the farmer's body for every year he serves him. He begins with the little finger, and does not give up before he has the whole body.

In a Norwegian legend, the nisse says that he has acquired seven souls on the farm and is expecting one more. He has been there for three generations. The husband's chair (in Hell) is already finished, the wife's chair is lacking a leg.

THE FOSSEGRIM

A tonal wizard

The *fossegrim* (or *grim*) is the musician among Norwegian spirits, and his instrument is the violin – or rather the *fiddle*. The nökk and the draug are also good fiddlers, but this is a secondary trait with them which, more often than not, has been borrowed from similar legends about the fossegrim. The grim is to be found at waterfalls and mills. It is especially on dark evenings that his playing can be heard. The fossegrim is not unwilling to teach his skills to others, and many a fiddler is said to have taken lessons from him. The pupil can contact him on a Thursday evening – now and then it is said *three* Thursday evenings in a row. With his face averted, he is to offer a white kid, and throw it into a waterfall that flows northwards. If the offering is too lean, the would-be-player merely learns how to *tune* his fiddle. But if the offering is nice and plump, the fossegrim seizes the pupil's hand and guides it back and forth across the strings until the blood spurts from his fingers. But then the pupil has served his apprenticeship, and can play so well that the trees start to dance and the waterfalls cease to flow. Here is a legend from Hallingdal:

The fossegrim is very fond of cured meat, and whenever anyone throws him some, he soon comes up on a stone out in the stream, with his fiddle, and plays for as short or as long a time, according to how big and good the piece of meat is.

If someone wanted to learn how to play from him, he had to take along a cured leg of mutton, which he threw in under the waterfall. After a while, the tiny little fellow shot up like an arrow and sat down on a stone with his fiddle in his hand. His hair was long and thick, and as yellow as gold. His nose and mouth were well-proportioned, and his eyes were as bright and shining as rock crystal. His hands were small and white, and his fingers moved so rapidly that you could not see them when he fingered his instrument. First he tuned his fiddle, and then he played it – sometimes so loudly that it rang, and sometimes softly and sweetly. And he kept on playing until the one who had thrown the meat had learned how to play. He then plunged into the water and was gone. But if there was too little meat on the bone, the one who had given it did not become much of a fiddler. If the joint were big and fat, he did better, and if some-one was generous enough to throw him a joint from a billygoat, he became a master fiddler.

There was once a scraper who wanted to learn how to play, but he could not bring himself to give the fossegrim a joint of meat. He wanted to go over to the waterfall without it, but everyone advised him not to, because they knew that the grim would not teach anyone well without payment. So he went down and looked over his meat, but the joints all seemed to be too big, and there wasn't one that he thought he could do with-out. Finally he took a leg from which the meat had been well-carved. This ought to be good enough, he thought. He threw the bone in the water and waited a long time before he saw the water-troll. At last he came – but not merrily and quickly, and he looked cross and out of sorts. Nonetheless, he started tuning his fiddle, but no playing came of it.

Then the lad was downhearted, and he said: 'I wanted to learn how to play.'

But the grim replied:

> '*I'll teach you to tune, now,*
> *but never to bow.*
> *You gave me a bone,*
> *but the meat was all gone.*'

One can also contact the fossegrim by taking along a leg of meat to a crossroads or a mill on Christmas Eve. The supernatural beings come at midnight. A swap is made. The fossegrim gets the joint, and the would-be-player gets a fiddle. And the fiddle is as good as the meat. And then the lesson begins. In the meantime, for some strange reason or other, the player must see to it that he is sitting the whole

time on a calfskin of a single color. It is sometimes said that the meat that is offered must not come from one's own storehouse. It must be stolen from another farm on the same evening. One learns how to play in such a way that everything that listens is compelled to dance: animals and people, even tables and chairs whirl about. And one learns how to tune the fiddle so high that the strings will break if anyone else tries to imitate it.

Some people say that not one but *three* teachers come, and the poorest teacher must receive the most meat. Ole Bull – the most celebrated violinist in Norway – is said to have learned how to play in this fashion.

Thursday night and Christmas Eve have been mentioned, but New Year's Night and Midsummer Night are also important. To be sure, an encounter with the grim seems to have been unpleasant. At Sundal, however, a meeting could be avoided. Here, it was enough to throw a shoulder of pork under the mill at midnight on Christmas night. If one did, one became a master fiddler.

It was not only unpleasant to meet the grim, it could be dangerous as well. No supernatural being can be trusted completely.

It happened that not everyone who tried, managed to learn anything.

Sigurd Nergaard, the folklorist, has recorded a long and colorful account from Österdal. Here is an excerpt from it:

There was a hired boy at Foss. He stole a leg of mutton, took along his fiddle and went down to the falls in the river. There he threw out the meat, and then he sat down and drew his bow across the strings. This was on a Thursday evening, but he did not notice anything. But the mistress of the farm came out however, and when she heard the playing down by the falls, she almost fainted. On the second evening, as he sat there, the river rose so high that the boy was almost carried away. And it was in *this* shape that the grim revealed itself. The boy became frightened and fled. He did not try on the third evening. And it was

probably a good thing he didn't, or else he would have been lost
by now.

If someone really wanted to become a fiddler, he only had to go and sit under a bridge by a stream, three Thursday evenings in a row. And he was to sit there and practice until daybreak. Then, if he went back on the fourth Thursday evening, someone would come and tell him what to do next.

Well, Ola sat under the bridge three Thursday nights in a row, and he practiced. Then he went back on the fourth Thursday and sat down. After a while, a tiny, little man came up – he was only a foot or two high. And he said he was now going to make Ola the best fiddler in all Norway, if he would give him his soul in return. Then Ola became frightened, he did, when he heard there was such devilment afoot. He said 'No,' then and there, and wanted to go. But the man told him to wait. If he did not want to agree to the bargain, there was nothing to be done about that. But he could still become a great fiddler. All he had to do was to kill a black cat and put it under the bridge for him. Well, if it wasn't anything worse than that, the boy would have been only too willing to do it. But he didn't think there was a black cat to be found in the parish, because no black kittens had been seen by anyone.

Well, there was yet another solution: He was to capture a snake and yank out its tongue, while it was still alive. Then he was to drop the tongue down in the fiddle and let the snake go again. At the same time, he was to gouge the right eye out of a living squirrel, and do the same with it. If he did all that, he would become a fine fiddler. Then the man was gone, and the boy stood there alone.

Well, it wasn't exactly a nice thing to do, but he wanted to be a fiddler so badly that he decided to try, because then he wouldn't be selling his soul to any man. So he rushed about the whole day looking for a squirrel – climbing trees, practically tearing his clothes to shreds. But when evening came, he had made no headway, and he was so tattered and torn that he decided not to follow this advice either.

In many places, the fossegrim was also called the *fossekall* or the *kvernknurr* – or perhaps he was mistaken for one of these spirits. As the kvernknurr, he appeared as something of a bogeyman. Here is a fragment of a legend from Hallingdal:

There was a man who was at the mill one night. But no one was supposed to stay there or let the mill grind after it was dark, because the grim became very angry if he did not get his night's rest. The man was aware of this, but he paid no attention to it. His only thought was to finish grinding his grain. When it was getting late, he heard a great smacking on the water, and then some tremendous blows on the walls – again and again. After a while, the door flew open, and the man caught sight of a skull that filled the entire doorway. The chin rested on the threshold, the brow reached the top of the door frame and the jawbones touched the sides. His eyes were as big as round tabletops, and his mouth was as black as pitch. The troll stood there for å while, glowering and gaping and shaking his head. Then he said, 'Now that was quite a skull, man!' The man was so terrified that he was at his wits' end. His only thought was to get out, but the door was jammed, and so he had to stay there the whole night. Sometimes the mill shook to and fro like a sieve, and, sometimes handfuls of meal were blown right in his eyes. But as day was dawning he got out at last, and he was on the point of running up the hill. But at that moment, one of the leather meal sacks landed on the back of his neck, knocking him off the path. He scrambled to his feet and took to his heels. Then he heard the grim shouting:

'I'm letting you go
with nary a mark.
But don't you come back here,
after it's dark!
Maybe the next time
your bones I will break –
Just to remind you,
you kept me awake!'

UGLY AS THE NÖKK

The hour has come but not the man

The *nökk* (or *nykk*) lives in lakes, ponds, rivers and high waterfalls. He was thought of as an old man with green eyes, big ears, and a long, full beard that drips with water as he emerges from the deep. An aura of eerieness surrounds him. According to an old ballad:

> *'The nökk lifts up his watery beard,*
> *and awaits his prey with longing.'*

He drags people down with him into the deep. It was said that every year he wanted at least one human offering. He was especially greedy for little children. Thus, it was customary to frighten disobedient children with the nökk – a sinister bogeyman, who was bound to take them if they played too close to the water ... for example, when they were going to pick 'nökke-roses' (waterlilies). But it is not until the sun goes down that he is really dangerous. Night belongs to the powers of evil.

To see or hear the nökk was a sign that someone was going to drown. Many people claimed to have heard the nökk shouting at places where people were drowned later in the year. And, like the draug, he shrieks at sea where there has been a shipwreck. In Denmark, when someone had drowned, it was said: 'The nökk has taken him away.' And if a drowned person was found with a red nose: 'The nökk has sucked him.' In Norway, if someone got a swelling on his leg after swimming in a river, it was sometimes called a 'nökk-bite.'

A distinctive type of legend has evolved around the nökk who lures people to him – or at least warns of their death. Here is an example from Hallingdal:

> On an isolated farm in a forest, not far from a creek, the household heard the nökk come up in a pool, shrieking so the forest rang: 'The hour has come but not the man!'
>
> Then some of the farmboys went down to the spot and hid in order to see what was going to happen.
>
> After a while, a man came along, and he was in such a hurry that the sweat poured off him – and he had to cross the creek. The boys were afraid that he was the one the nökk had been calling for, and so they grabbed the man and held onto him for dear life. But he cried and carried on, because he had to go across the creek – come what might. All the same, they did not let him go. But then the farmer told them to give him some water. If he were meant to die, he would die all the same. But if he weren't, then it wouldn't harm him in the least.
>
> Well, they acted accordingly. But no sooner had the man taken a sip of water than he dropped dead on the spot, and it turned out that the nökk had prophesied correctly.

The nökk is no beauty, but, like the utburd, he is able to change himself into any shape he likes – an ability he makes frequent use of, as well he might. Whenever he warns that someone is going to drown, he sometimes appears in the shape of a bird, and sits shrieking on the surface of the water. He is also reported to have changed himself into half a boat, half a horse, and, when night has fallen, into various precious objects of gold or silver. If someone picks the treasure up in his hands, the nökk has him in his power and drags him down into the water with him. At Lake Erte, in Römskog, the nökk was once eccentric enough to disguise himself as a naked man – how he was recognized, the legend does not say. We are reminded of the river-troll from Jæren – a naked man who hops about on one foot. At Sunnmöre, this same troll is known by the name of *Hopperten* ('The Hopper'), because he can make a hop a mile and a half long. But, on the other hand, the sole of his foot is as big as the bottom of a bushel barrel. We are not going to

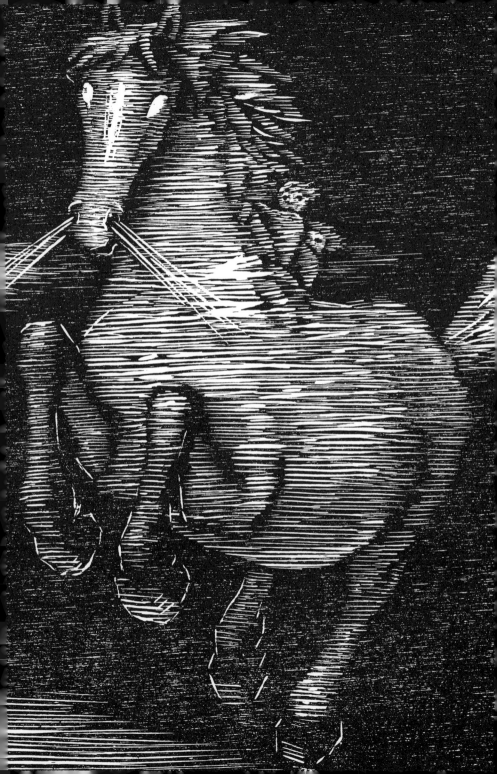

accuse the nökk and Hopperten of being identical, but their interest in nudism and the outdoor life is obviously mutual.

It is most common, however, for the nökk to transform himself into a horse. Here is a legend from Österdal:

> Three little boys were busy playing down by the river, when a grey horse came up out of the water and lay down in their midst. Now, you know how little boys are – they're always up to something – and so it wasn't long before the two oldest had scrambled up on the horse's back.
>
> Then the youngest boy came: 'I got here in the *nick* of time,' he said.
>
> But then the horse sprang to his feet with the two boys on his back, and headed out into the river with a mighty splash.
>
> Thus it was the nökk that had changed himself into a horse. He had probably intended to take all three of the boys with him, but got scared when he thought he heard his name.

Like so many other spirits, the nökk loses his powers when he is recognized or called by his correct name.

According to Andreas Faye, some sort of a monster is supposed to have dwelled in Fyris Lake, in Telemark. 'And every time there is a storm, or bad weather is brewing,' wrote Faye, 'it appears in the shape of a big horse, rearing up in the water on its enormous hooves. Rore Lake, in Nedenes, was also supposed to have been haunted by a troll which appeared now as a horse, now as a load of hay, now as a serpent, and even once as a crowd of people. But to what extent this Rore troll can truly be called a *nökk* is an open question.

On the other hand, it really was a nökk at Sunnmöre that changed itself into a mitten – or perhaps it was a being so tiny that there was *room* for it in the thumb of a mitten. Unfortunately, a not too fastidious cow was present and devoured the mitten. Long afterwards, the nökk could be heard shouting from the cow's stomach: 'Open up! Let me out!' And in the end the cow had to be slaughtered.

Things can turn out equally as badly for the nökk, if he
should happen to run into a parson of the really old school
– or any other knowledgeable men, for that matter. Here
are two examples collected by Andreas Faye around the be-
ginning of the 19th century:

'Even though the nökk is a dangerous troll, he sometimes
meets his match. According to legend, there lived a nökk in
Sund Rapids at Gjerrestad, who was often responsible for people
losing their lives as they rowed up or down the rapids, as was
the custom. The parson, who was apprehensive of this nökk,
took along four stalwart fellows. Twice he had them row up the
rapids with all their might, but they glided back each time
without coming all the way up. When they rowed up the third
time, the men saw the parson reach down in the water at the
head of the rapids and grab something with his hand. He drew
up a black creature which resembled a little black dog. The
parson told the men to continue rowing, up to the lake. He held
the nökk firmly between his feet, and remained quite silent.
When they approached the rockslide at Tvet, he conjured the
nökk under the stones. Since that time, no one has drowned in
the rapids. But, on the other hand, two people have drowned at
the rockslide – where the sound of wailing, as if from people in
mortal danger, can still be heard.
    The nökk at Bahus fared no better. He changed himself into
a horse at Morland, and walked along the shore to graze. But a
wise man, who thought something was amiss, cast a bridle over
him. And it was so cunningly made that he could not get loose
again. The man now kept the nökk with him the whole spring,
and really tormented him by using him to plow all his fields.
Finally the bridle came loose by accident, and, like a flash, the
nökk plunged into the lake, dragging the harrow with him.

We also find the nökk in many different guises in Sweden – now a grown man (a dangerous 'lady-killer'), or as a
handsome youth – but with the body of a horse from the
waist down; or as an old man, or even as a little boy, wearing a red cap over golden ringlets. On calm summer evenings, the boy sits on the glassy surface of the water with a
golden harp in his hands.

8 – Phantoms.

The nökk as a musician is a favorite motif in Norway, even though music is usually associated with the *fossegrim*. But the nökk's music is almost always *sinister*. It probably sounds pretty to the listener, but it is being played in order to lure people into the water where the nökk can capture them.

A man by the name of Israel, from Sör-Odal, is supposed to have seen the nökk sitting on a rock in the middle of the lake, playing on a golden harp. Israel quickly made the sign of the cross three times on his forehead with his finger, in order to keep the nökk from getting him.

In all fairness, a more sympathetic branch of the tradition should also be mentioned: during the winter, the nökk is sitting on the bottom of an ice-covered lake, waiting for spring. He can than be heard sighing heavily. But during the summer he is light-hearted and gay. He then plays on his harp in the waterfall. Indeed, the more the water tumbles about him, the more merrily he plays. But, as has been said, this is a *most* sympathetic description of an otherwise forbidding water-troll. The nökk is not only a harpist, he also knows how to handle a violin bow. And with that, we are encroaching dangerously close onto the professional domain of another spirit – the fossegrim.

In conclusion – how did one protect oneself from the nökk? We have already learned the most important remedy – that is, calling him by name. At Mo, the following formula was said:

> '*Nykke, Nykke, needle in the water,*
> *The Virgin Mary throws steel in the water,*
> *You sink, I'll run...*'

In Ofoten, it was said that the nökk usually kept to the cloudberry marshes. Before picking the first berry, one was supposed to say: 'Nökk! Nökk! Nökk!' Otherwise, one could be captured.

In Helgeland, whenever someone lay down to drink from a stream, he said: 'Ptooey! Troll at the bottom/ Cross in the water/ Leave me be/ To each his own/ God for me!'

In Sweden, great care was taken to keep human blood and urine from coming into a brook, because then the nøkk or the elves could bewitch it. Here too, people used to spit in front of them before drinking from a brook, otherwise the nökk could harm them. If one let one's horse drink from a lake, it was necessary to spit in the water first, otherwise the nökk could transform the horse. And of course one had to spit whenever one went across water.

In Hedmark, people were a bit more pious. Here they always said, 'In Jesus' name', if they went across running water after the sun had gone down, because, according to the tradition: 'There is so much evil in the water.'

THE OSKOREI

The terrifying host

The *oskorei* is a great company of men and women who – with an infernal racket – ride or drive about the country-side at night, just before and during Christmas. (For this reason, in many places, they are also called the *jolerei* – the 'Yuletide host'). They ride over land and water. Indeed, they can even journey through the air. Wherever they go they spread terror and horror.

It is uncertain what the name *oskorei* means. Many people have thought that is it *ásgoðreið* or *ásguðreið*, i.e. 'Aasgaard's Ride' – a company of the ancient Norse gods. But today there is a tendency to accept Ivar Aasen's definition, and connect the name with the Old Norse *Oskur* ('terror'), in *Oskurlegr*, and then the definition should be 'the terrifying host'.

A number of features of the oskorei-legends suggest that the host was made up of ghosts. In Telemark, it was believed that the host consisted of those who were undeserving of both Heaven and Hell.

With jangling iron bridles, uttering loud shrieks and cries, the oskorei swoops across the sky – a whirlwind so fast that it is often impossible to make out details. As a rule, they ride on horses – black horses, with eyes that shine in the dark and glow like embers – but other animals can also be used. At Roligheden, a cottar's holding in Søgne in Southern Norway, it is said that the oskorei stole a big cock and rode on that. According to another account, the steeds of the oskorei look exactly like empty barrels.

Nonetheless, horses are the most common – some are their own horses, and some are stolen from farms through

which the oskorei passes. For this reason, it was necessary
to hang steel over the doors and draw the sign of the cross
on the doors with chalk or tar.

If a horse would not eat on Christmas Eve, it was a sure
sign that the oskorei had taken it. The real horse was now
beyond the blue horizon. The one that remained in the
stable was only a likeness. The horse was gone, the skin remained. It then was necessary to let a tallow candle smoke
under its nostrils, and the real horse would immediately return, dripping with sweat – proof that it had run with the
oskorei.

People can also be carried off in the same way:

'At Vallstad, in Fyrisdal, the family was sitting quietly on
Christmas Eve. But, before they knew what was happening, a
girl, who was sitting there with them, started acting very strangely.
She suddenly started moving her arms and legs as if she were
holding the reins of a skittish horse, and riding it: trot, trot,
trot! Suddenly she fell over backwards and lay the whole night
as if she were dead. It was no use touching her, because the
oskorei had carried her off with them. She came to again in the
morning, and then she told them that she had been riding so
hard with the oskorei that – even when they had ridden across
Lake Fyris – the sparks had showered from the horseshoes as if
they had been riding on a plain of the hardest rock. She had also
dropped in at various farms with the host and had partaken of
food and drink. Her hair ribbon was found hanging from the
chimney. The girl was light-hearted and gay, and an excellent
singer and dancer, and this is the kind of person the oskorei
like to get hold of. But most of all, they want to get hold of
bullies and brawlers and the like, who make a lot of noise and
trouble.

From Telemark, M. B. Landstad has also written down
a description of the participants in this demonic ride. Seen
from the front, they are stalwart and fair, he says, but from
the rear they are hollow like a trough or a hollow aspen
tree. At the head of the procession rides *Guro Rysserova*
(Mare's tail). She is big and hideous. Her horse is black

and is called *Skokse*. Guro's husband is called *Sigurd*. He is so decrepit and infirm that he has to have help opening and closing his eyes. His horse is called *Grane*.

From other parts of the country, it was also reported that a woman rides at the head. She is supposed to have two dogs with her, and when she passes through the farms, she allows them to run into the houses and beg for food. But they are not permitted to steal – a bit of information that does not tally with what we otherwise know about the oskorei's behavior. .

They say that the Jularei has two dogs with her, and when she passes through the farms she lets them go in the houses to get some food, but she won't hear of them stealing. Now it happened that one of the dogs had gone into a cottage while the people were out, and there he started to drink some milk that was standing in a wooden bowl on the bench. But all at once the people came in. They started to beat the dog. The Julerei heard him yelping and so she called to him:
'What's the matter with Votte?' she said.
'Votte's been caught', he replied ('Votte' was the dog's name).
'What has he done wrong, then?' she asked.
'Oh, he took a drop of milk,' he said.
'Did he now?' she said. 'Then it's a good thing he's getting a beating. He'll get one from me too.'

In Northern Norway, people readily told about an outlawed woman who roamed about in the air. Her name was Melusina, and every Saturday she turned into a fish from the waist down. In order to conceal this, she left home every weekend. But her husband began to suspect that she was unfaithful, and one Saturday he followed her. In this way he discovered her secret handicap. Well, had he held his tongue about what he knew, everything would have been all right. But because he gave her away, she was outlawed, and she has roamed restlessly about in the air ever since.

In Hardanger, the oskorei is described as a company of black men with long tails and wings like enormous bearskins.

Others believe that hulders and hidden people are the ones who ride about in this fashion. Some people think that the oskorei is a bewitched bridal procession, and a few have made a guess that it is Herod's daughter and her offspring – or perhaps 'The Five Foolish Virgins'.

There is also an account in which the participants are described as very tiny people, about the size of 4–6 year old boys. The boys are black and wear black knitted caps – and the horses they ride are also black – of course.

The oskorei dropped in at the farms wanting to taste the Christmas fare. It was especially important to protect the Christmas ale from them. It helped to fasten a sheath knife to each hoop of the brewing vat, and to make the sign of the cross on every beer barrel. Many people used to place a bucket of water in front of the barrels. The Oskorei usually tastes the first thing it finds. If it gets hold of the bucket of water, it merely says, 'Fie!' and goes away. It is even better to use a pail of tar. Then the oskorei slams the door and will not go inside at all. Not only is the freshly brewed ale in danger. At Bygland, in Setesdal, it was maintained that the oskorei was able (through the art of magic) to tap the ale directly from the grain, and so it was necessary to protect *that* too.

But steel and the sign of the cross were not only supposed to protect the horses and the Christmas food. People were mostly concerned about their own lives. It is no joke to be carried away by the oskorei. There are tremendous forces at work here. Even huge boulders fly through the air. In a gust of wind, the oskorei can sweep straight through the house, and lift the beams so the sun shines through the chinks. People are snatched away, body and soul, no matter if they are out walking or sitting by the table or the bench.

Many of them are never found again. In Setesdal it was said outright that whoever was taken by the oskorei was killed at the next unsaddling place.

In Kvitseid, the people on a farm had been to a feast. While they were away, they had left the food standing on the table, as was the custom at Christmas-time. When they came home, they discovered that the oskorei had been there and had greedily helped themselves. And a dead man was hanging in the parlor. He was wearing clothes that revealed that he had come from Numedal. In all likelihood, the oskorei had carried him along with them from Numedal, and either he had been murdered there in the room or else he had ridden himself to death during the hard riding.

Grotesque, too, is the story that Landstad has recorded from a farm in Vraadal:

It happened once at Lofthus, in Vraadal, that the Aasgaardreid played a dirty trick on Peer. There was a shepherd boy at the farm whose name was Peer. As was to be expected, he was the last one to have a bath on Christmas Eve. But Peer was gone for such a long time that they started wondering where he was. He was supposed to carry in wood and put it under the cauldron. But Peer never came. At last they went to see what had become of him, but when they were almost out by the bathhouse, they could hear a man's voice inside. It was someone with a gruff voice who was slowly chanting in a singsong voice:

> *'Pickin' at Peer in the bathhouse here*
> *Pickin' at Peer in the bathhouse here ...'*

They became frightened and dared not go inside. Then too, it was very late. After a while, they went out again to listen, but they still heard the same thing:

> *'Pickin' at Peer in the bathhouse here,*
> *Pickin' at Peer in the bathhouse here ...'*

No one dared go inside before morning, and then Peer was found torn to shreds. It was the Aasgaardreid that had been picking' at him.

Most people protected themselves against the oskorei, and tried to shut it out. Others gave up, and tried to appease the oskorei instead – they put out food for it, yes, even decked the table for the ghosts.

Nonetheless, the best thing to do was to put up a struggle, to protect oneself as well as possible. In many parts of the country it was said that the one who has food on hand needs not fear the oskorei. Then one is able to save not only oneself, but also the unfortunate people who had been forced to ride along in the ghostly company. A woman once saved a man by holding a basket of food over his head. Then the oskorei had to let him go.

It has also happened that people have escaped by *throwing* food to the oskorei. A woman was on her way from the bakehouse with an armful of cakes, when she was attacked. Resolutely, she threw a cake up in the air, and while the oskorei ate it, she escaped into the house.

If someone had been captured by the oskorei, he still had a chance. If the host went over a field of stubble as it continued on its way, then it had to let him go.

A field of stubble also offers protection to anyone who happens to be standing there. And if one is able to run into such a field, then one is saved. It also helps to be standing at a crossroads. Another good remedy is to hurry home and look inside the oven, but, as a rule, one is unable to come that far.

This story takes place during the summer. It is an exception. As a rule, the oskorei appears during the dark time of the year:

A man from Natadal had been over in Hjartdal, and so it happened that it was late in the afternoon when he started for home. By the time he had come to Anbjörn Valley the sun had set, and when he had come up on the mountain at Valler, on his way toward Blengs Valley, it was the quietest of summer nights and not a single bird was chirping any longer. As he walked there, he heard a terrible commotion behind him. He turned around to see what it was, and realized it was the oskorei who were rushing along. Bridles jingled and weapons clinked, and he heard them talking and quarreling among themselves. The oskorei wanted food, and Guro their leader said they would have to wait until they came to Natadal. There they would eat

their fill, both they and their horses, for there they would find
'Friday-baked bread and Sunday-raked hay!'

When the Natadal man heard this, he did not feel any too comfortable, for they were talking about his own storehouse and haymow. But now the oskorei were so close behind him that there was no chance of running away. He ran off the road a little way and, flinging himself down on the grass on his back, he stretched his arms straight out on each side so that he was lying there in the shape of a cross.

When Guro came up, she stopped and shrieked: 'Ugh! Look at that cross!'

Then they dared not ride past him, but went a long way around. When the man saw this, he jumped up and took to his heels as fast as he could. He had a slight headstart and hurried home. He managed to make a sign of the cross above the wicket in the road down to the farm and on all the doors. Guro was thereby cheated out of food and drink and dared not ride in to the farm.

In the old days, Friday was a day of fasting, and no work was to be done in which a swinging or rolling movement was involved. Therefore, they could not bake flat-bread. And on Sunday one was neither supposed to mow nor to rake hay. It was a sin to work, and the evil powers had the right to take the fruits of this labor. This was why Guro had placated her company by saying that at Natadal they would find Friday-baked bread and Sunday-raked hay. And she would have found it too, if the man had not placed the sign of the cross in her way.

When the oskorei passes a man who has lain down on the ground with his arms outstretched in the shape of a cross, every single one in the company spits on him. When the entire oskorei has passed, the man, in turn, must remember to spit after *them*. Otherwise he can easily suffer permanent injury.

The fact that the sign of the cross is strong meat for witchcraft and the powers of evil, is apparent in a legend from Dalen, in Telemark, which is about a woman who made the sign of the cross in the air against the oskorei. At once, the ghostly riders were transformed into wooden logs that fell down and rolled along the ground.

124   In more recent times, the oskorei, like many other spirits, has deteriorated into something used to scare children with. In Sogn it is said that, on Christmas Eve, the oskorei goes from farm to farm in order to see if all the children are clean. If they are not, the oskorei carries them to a lake and drops them in.